THE GOOD GIRL

MADELEINE TAYLOR

1

I've never done this before. My legs tremble as I walk down the long hotel corridor. Her room is right at the very end; a suite, she told me. *Room 935.* I know the number will be etched in my memory forever, because as much as I want this, right now, I'm also terrified.

I left the bar shortly after her, needing one more drink for liquid courage before I got changed into the black satin dress I'd thankfully brought along. Besides the fact that it will come off easily, the idea of her running a hand up my thigh while I'm still wearing it excites me. My black heels sink into the carpet as I make my way to the point of no return, and I feel myself getting wet, my mind in the gutter at the thought of finally being touched again.

This certainly wasn't part of my plan when I woke up this morning. I'm a career-driven sales manager from Arizona, the highlight of my week being dinner with my parents every Sunday. Apart from that, I work long days and spend most nights alone in bed with my subscription of Netflix. My company's annual New York trip is always a refreshing change of scenery, as I love the city and I've been looking forward to coming here for weeks. The first day of the textiles trade show in the Financial District was busy as always, with vendors from all over the world promoting their latest fabrics.

The company I work for has a stand too, showcasing our organic cottons from Phoenix, where we are based. My job is demanding, and I travel a lot in between the office and our factory, which is one of the reasons I'm still single at thirty-five, or so I tell my friends. Deep down, I know that's not the case, though. Relationships have never been my priority. Perhaps because I'm ambitious and have been working my way up the corporate ladder for the past fifteen years, or perhaps because I've only come out to my close family and a handful of old friends, who I hardly ever see anymore. I never let anything get serious but not because I'm scared; I've just never met anyone I wanted to go through all that trouble for. Besides all the questions and opinions that I know will follow, it's simply no one's business.

It's been a while since I've been with a woman, and almost six months since my last girlfriend broke up with me because I wasn't 'invested'. I guess she was right. I wasn't, but I still miss the sex and I wonder if that's why I was so drawn to the woman on whose door I'm about to knock. She oozed sex; I could feel it, even from a distance.

We got talking in the bar of the hotel where most of the trade show delegates are staying, as it's conveniently situated right next door to the venue. While catching up with colleagues from different branches of my company, and a couple of buyers I'm hoping to write an order for, I was surprised to see a woman I didn't recognize watching me from the far end of the bar. Stepping away from the conversation, I smiled at her, trying to figure out if I knew her, or if she was involved in the organization of the show. My memory is exceptional, and although nothing about her rang a bell, my interest peaked at her intense stare. Smiling back, she gave me a nod and then beckoned me over. Curiously, I came as if I had no free will; I was just so instantly drawn to her. She was very attractive, handsome, and a bit older than me, I guessed. Short, messy hair, a killer smile and dimples that stirred something lascivious inside me. Her ultra-confident air made me think she was successful with the ladies, but mostly it was her attitude that drew me in. Slightly butch perhaps, she acted as if she already had me in the palm of her hand, and for some reason that excited me, but I can't deny that I was nervous as I approached. Subconsciously, I fiddled with my necklace, like I always do when I'm not entirely at ease. The cross around my neck holds no meaning to me any more in a religious sense, but it reminds me of where I came from, who I am, and it gives me a strange sense of comfort, just because it's always been there.

"What are you drinking?" she asked, placing her hand possessively on the small of my back as I joined her at the bar. It was a bold move, and she didn't pull it away after I'd taken a seat next to her. I could feel her warmth through my thin white shirt, and I think that's when I slowly started going crazy. Her hand casually curled around my waist, waking up body parts I'd neglected since my last girlfriend, or perhaps a part of me I never knew existed. The firm, confident, hold told me she was not afraid to take charge and although I'd never felt a need for previous girlfriends to do that, I liked it way more than I could have anticipated.

"Gin and tonic," I answered, swallowing hard. Her eyes were so blue, and they seemed to pierce right through me, to read every inch of desire that had been buried deep for months, years even.

"Gin and tonic. I like that," she said, licking her lips as she stared at my mouth. "You're sexy, you know that?"

"Right." I rolled my eyes, knowing there was nothing sexy about the way I looked, but the comment still made me feel slightly feverish and caused an ache to form between my thighs. My blonde hair was pulled back into a braid and I was wearing jeans, Nikes and a plain, white organic cotton blouse that hung frumpily from my shoulders. Being in charge of the Cotton Innovation Department, I'm expected to dress in line with our product offer. I can't say I love what they give me to wear for work, but since the main part of my job consists of interacting with clients, outward communications and promoting our brand, I don't really have a choice. By now, I'm so used to it that it's become a part of me and besides, I like my job and I don't have much else in my life, so I tend to do whatever they want me to. My trade show lanyard was still hanging around my neck as I turned to her, giving away my name. She tugged at it, pulling me closer, and I let her.

"Emily Evans." The way she said it could have passed for an orgasm coming from her mouth, and I think I gasped for a brief second as she pulled me closer to her enticing lips. Her breath was on my face as she looked deep into my lust filled eyes. "Emily Evans, would you like to come to my room?"

Even if I'd wanted to resist, my whole body reacted to her voice, her strong grip and her words in a way that was entirely new to me. No one had ever left me shaking on my feet just by using words alone, and honestly, I was fascinated.

"For what?" I asked, quietly cursing myself for sounding

so naïve. I looked around to make sure no one was listening in on our conversation. There would be a lot of gossip if my colleagues knew I was flirting with a woman. No one here knew about this part of me.

"Don't play innocent with your beautiful icy-gray eyes, you know exactly what I mean." Her tone was dominant as she took my drink from the bartender and handed it to me. "I want to fuck you, Emily. I want to make you feel like you've never felt before."

"How are you so sure you can do that?" My words didn't sound one bit convincing, but I said them anyway. I think I tore the lanyard back out of her hand at this point and straightened in an attempt to pull myself together, but it all then became a bit of a blur from there.

"You'll just have to wait and see." She paused and smiled at me and God, I swear, in that moment, I melted. "I'll see you in my suite, room number 935. In an hour." It was a command rather than a request, and after the way my body reacted to her only moments ago, how could I say no?

I'm still not sure if I'll go through with this as I stop in front of the door and hesitate. It's not too late to turn back, I think to myself. I'm a good girl. I don't go into strangers' hotel rooms and let them have their way with me. Instead, I tend to play it safe. I date women I meet online, more out of boredom than anything else, and the dates sometimes turn into relationships. I usually feel suffocated after a while and become distant which eventually drives them away. It's a ridiculously complex way to get laid, I realize then. Before I have the chance to change my mind, the door unlocks, and she opens it for me with a look that tells me she knew I'd bite.

"You came," she says, never taking her eyes off me. She's

wearing a white hotel branded robe and it seems that, like me, she's just had a shower.

"I did." Has she been waiting for me behind the door? Did she sense my hesitation? My fear? Strangely, that thought arouses me even more as I step inside her suite.

2

The room is spacious and luxurious, and I wonder what she does for a living. We never got past the brief introduction at the bar before she offered her indecent proposal—which I apparently was happy to accept—but right now, I kind of like the mystery of not knowing. She follows me through the short corridor which holds a closet and small kitchenette, and we end up in the bedroom that is decorated in neutral tones and rich fabrics. The enormous four-poster bed dominates the left side of the room and on the right is a lounge area, big enough to comfortably seat six, with a cocktail cabinet next to it. Long, silk cream colored curtains are open on either side of the floor-to-ceiling windows and, even though it's unlikely that anyone will see us up here, I get the feeling she likes the thought of being exposed. The lights are dimmed to perfection and there's a cooler with Champagne and two glasses on one of the mahogany nightstands. I can feel her presence behind me and hold my breath as she inches closer.

"Are you okay, Emily?" she asks. Her voice is low and sultry.

"I think so," I whisper. "What's your name?" I ask, thinking how ridiculous the question sounds. I didn't know her name an hour ago and I'm still here, but I want to know.

"Call me whatever you want." The answer lingers in my ear. Her lips are against it, warm and wet, as she wraps an arm around my waist from behind. It's almost tender, but when she pulls me closer against her, I can feel her need – a desire that is so strong, it is nothing short of carnal. I almost go limp in her arms as I try to remember to breathe. There's something hard pushing against my backside and I freeze for a moment when I reach behind me and feel a silicone dildo poking against my ass. My heart races in my chest, knowing what's coming.

"I'm going to fuck you." She breathes heavily into my ear as she speaks and all I can do is nod. I feel her hands roam over my silk clad breasts and when she gropes them possessively and kisses my neck, a throaty moan passes my lips. I have no experience with strap-ons. A rather boring good girl like me doesn't tend to be adventurous in bed, but even though I'm a little apprehensive, there's nothing I want more right now. My black lace panties are soaked from my juices, the excitement of this moment causing a pool to form between my legs, and I need her to rip them off me.

"Then do it," I say, and turn around to face her. Her eyes darken as she leans in to kiss me and my craving for her grows to explosive proportions when she parts her lips and claims me with her tongue. It's so intense, so incredibly sexy that I squirm as our mouths melt together into a wild kiss. I reach up to run my hands through her hair. It's still damp from her shower and smells of citrus. Her lips pull into a smile against mine as she backs me up against the wall and presses herself hard against me. Having her body against mine sends a powerful rush through me, and for a moment,

I'm afraid I'm going to explode from the pressure against my crotch.

"Tell me if you want me to stop," she whispers, then takes my mouth again in a kiss that leaves me dizzy and so turned on that I can't even think straight. She's a great kisser; deep, possessive, passionate. *Fuck.* Just like I imagined, she slides a hand under my dress. I nearly come just from anticipation alone and many unspoken questions start to run through my mind. *'How does she do this? Why do I feel like I'm about to climax already? Is it just the thrill of being with a stranger and if so, why haven't I tried this sooner?'* The muscles in my legs tremble and I wrap my arms around her broad shoulders to help me stay up as she traces the inside of my thigh upward with her fingers, she then gropes my dripping center and squeezes me hard. I let out another moan, louder this time, and it seems to inspire her. Her other hand reaches behind me to pull down the zipper of my dress. When I step out of it, I'm only wearing a black lace lingerie set and my heels. The silver cross suddenly feels heavy around my neck and I reach for the clasp to take it off and drop it to the ground. Even with my eyes closed now, as I try to compose myself and catch my breath, I can feel her watching me. I know she can smell my excitement, can see it from the way my chest heaves up and down abnormally fast like a trapped animal. And I know she's enjoying this.

Before her hand reaches into the front of my panties, I give her an almost invisible nod, letting her know I want nothing more than her hand there. I gasp when her fingers slide through my drenched pussy, exploring me. Her touch feels shattering, explosive and so right, as if I've been waiting for it all my life. She moves down and dips inside me, just a little, never taking her eyes off mine. They're darker now, more sapphire blue, and the longing I see in them doesn't lie; she wants me just as much as I want her.

"God you're so wet," she says in between breaths. I know I am. In fact, I don't think I've ever been this turned on before. Her other hand unclasps my bra and she yanks it off me, the lust written all over her face as she tosses it behind her. She takes in my small breasts before her lips mold greedily around my taut nipples. They are hard, so hard, and the contact with her wet and warm mouth makes me suck in a quick breath as my pussy clenches around her skilled fingers.

"Take me," I beg, and I mean it. It's all I want.

"Lie down." She whispers her command as she takes a step back and gestures toward the bed.

'This is not me,' I think to myself. 'This is not like me at all, following orders.' But I still do it. I crave it. On unsteady legs, I move to the imposing bed, fall back on top of the covers and watch her come toward me. The black dildo is sticking jauntily out of her robe, but it doesn't frighten me anymore. Tonight, it's an extension of her and even though she's a stranger, I can sense she would never hurt me. She just wants to make me feel good - like she told me earlier, and I believe her. I know she gets off on this, I can see the desire in her eyes. The fire in mine must be visible too because she gives me another smile. By now, her approval feels like a reward and it's so sexy that I hardly dare to look as she takes hold of my panties and slowly pulls them down my legs. Her lips part for a split second as she looks down on me and I see a throb in the vein at the base of her neck, but she quickly regains control, takes off her robe and lowers herself on top of me. I shudder as I feel her body, her warm skin, her soft breasts as they press down on mine. I'd say that I've had my fair share of good sex, but this is a whole new sensation and unlike anything I've ever felt before. Aroused is an understatement. All my senses are heightened, every nerve-ending on high alert to the point that they're oversensitive.

She spreads my legs apart with her thighs and runs a finger through my wetness again, teasing me as she licks my lips and wedges her tongue between them, kissing me in the most sensual way. I'm aware of the liquid desire that has gathered between my legs as she slowly pushes a finger inside of me, then adds another one. I'm wet and throbbing and almost delirious when her thumb brushes over my engorged clit.

"You're so tight," she mumbles against my mouth, and the comment makes me squirm underneath her. She retracts her probing fingers while her lips stay locked with mine and places the silicon shaft between my legs, then hooks her arm under my knee and lifts it, before she slowly eases herself in, little by little. I moan, then hold my breath and moan again, louder. I clearly need this, I need her right now, and that's crazy because I don't even know her name.

"Are you okay?" she asks again. There's something strangely attentive about her voice. Something that wasn't there a minute ago when all I heard was pure, lecherous desire.

"Yes," I say, pulling her in closer. Her weight feels perfect on top of me as she fills me up, stretching me, and I'm trying hard to stay in the present because it's so easy to slip into ecstasy. I want this to last, and I want to remember everything tomorrow. Every touch, every kiss, every thrust, every look... Her thumb parts my lips and she studies my face while I wallow in pleasure. I suck her digit into my mouth and a flash of satisfaction hits my core when I hear her moan too. It drives me wild. My legs wrap tightly around her hips when she starts moving in and out of me, slowly at first, then faster as I buck my hips, my body begging for more because I'm already close. So close. Just as I'm seconds away from losing myself, she pulls out of me and shakes her head, giving me a teasing smile.

"Not so fast." She lifts her hips and steadies herself on her knees, making sure not to touch anything below my waist because I'm so sensitive that even the slightest pressure will make me come. "I want you to beg for it. You can't come until I tell you to."

I look up at her with disbelief because I'm throbbing and so desperate that I'd probably offer up a body part for her to continue. But her teasing is also incredibly sexy, and I can't deny that I like her being in control. "Please, can I come?" I ask through ragged breaths.

"No." She tilts her head and catches my hands as they travel down her waist in an attempt to pull her closer, then pins them above my head. "Not yet." Her mouth meets mine again and I know she's close too; I can feel her trembling despite her outward appearance of self-restraint. Arching my back, I invite her to move to my breasts and she instinctively does, sucking at my nipple. It feels so good that I buck my hips against hers, seeking something, anything.

"Please fuck me and make me come," I beg once more, and this time, she seems to give in to my lewd request as she moves back up to my mouth and slowly enters me again with the strap-on.

"Good girl," she says in a hoarse voice as she starts fucking me deep and hard. "Come with me."

It's all it takes to send me over the edge. Her hands catch mine again, lacing our fingers together. For some reason, that simple action feels more intimate than anything I've ever done, but I don't care because a storm starts brewing in my lower abdomen, sending waves of ecstasy through my entire body. I feel high, euphoric, I'm glowing, and I cry out when my walls contract around her. My head falls back against the pillows and I can feel her eyes on me as I almost drown in bliss. Instinctively, my hands want to reach for her face and draw her down into a kiss, but she's still holding them in her tight grip when she reaches release herself and climaxes with a loud cry. I love the sound of her letting go.

"Kiss me." I'm breathing fast, barely able to get the words out. She releases my hands, takes off the harness, and almost tenderly, wipes a strand of blonde hair from my forehead. I'm sweating and so is she; I can taste the salt on her mouth as she brushes her lips against mine. As my body starts to relax, I wonder what the hell just happened. '*Who is she?*' I lace my fingers through her hair and pull her into a slow and lazy kiss, cherishing her taste while I still can. "What's your name?" I mumble, because now I can't seem to stop obsessing about it.

"May," she says, and I know she's lying.

3

My lack of sleep is wearing me down today, as I sit in our company booth at the textile trade show. There are three big rooms with vendors, and my colleague Jeff and I only have tomorrow left to work our way through the wealth of fabrics our competitors are offering in between our meetings on the stand.

Currently having a free minute to myself, I cast a quick glance at the paperwork on the chair beside me, then decide to ignore it. On Monday, I'll be giving a presentation on a new lightweight cotton denim that our company is launching next month. My speech is intended to inspire buyers to try it, to use it for their collections and it's a big opportunity for me. If it reaches the anticipated success it's supposed to, I can see another promotion for me in the near future. I've worked hard on the launch and this is the first reveal of the material that looks just like denim but is ten times lighter, meaning it provides ultimate comfort for casual wear. I've been so busy catching up on other projects I'm leading that I haven't had time to prepare for the presentation yet, and last night didn't give me much opportunity to write the speech either. I doubt I'd be able to concentrate if I tried and tell myself that I still have another day to do it.

Secretly, I'm hoping I'll see her again, though, and the flashbacks of last night are seriously distracting me. Her hands all over me, her mouth on mine, her body raging with need as she came on top of me... Perhaps that was the highlight of my night, hearing her curse my name. I wish I'd tasted her, because now I have a raging thirst that needs to be quenched and it's all I can think of.

I couldn't sleep when I got back to my room, still a little freaked out by my out-of-character behavior. She didn't ask me to leave, but I sensed that she wanted to be alone, and so I left in the middle of the night, exhausted but extremely satisfied. I guess satisfied is an understatement, as I could probably live on the memory alone for the coming five years. Despite my fatigue, I feel like a different woman, like I'd found a key to some secret place inside me that I didn't know existed. As much as my sexual awakening thrills me, it also makes me question many things. For years, I thought I knew myself on a sexual level, but I clearly didn't. Why did it excite me so much when she told me what to do? And why do my thoughts keep telling me that I want to do it all again? That I want to give myself to her, to be consumed over and over?

"Feel this, Em." Jeff walks into our stand and hands me a swatch he's found at one of our competitors.

Taking it, I run my fingers over the fabric and study the swatch. "Impressive." It is impressive indeed, to the touch especially, but I have other things on my mind. *'Is she still at the hotel?'* I wanted to ask how long she was here for before I left her room, but as I didn't expect an answer, I didn't bother. Now I regret not enquiring about her stay because the thought of never seeing her again bothers me more as each hour passes. I check my phone; it's four pm. Going back to the hotel now to see if she's there will surely raise suspicion with Jeff and I still have one more client to see, so I shrug it off and make some notes on the swatch instead. After all, this is what I live for and last night was only a fleeting moment. Apart from physical pleasure, and perhaps some new insights on my side, it meant nothing to me, and I'm pretty sure that it meant nothing to her. As my thoughts come and go, I know I'm fooling myself because I have not been able to think of anything but her since I left her room. More than anything, I want to repeat the encounter and that scares me. Am I obsessed? It's likely. I've never felt this compulsive need to see someone again. My sexual encounters usually just evolve out of habit and I'm never the instigator if a relationship goes beyond a one-night stand. Her mouth flashes before me and I feel an urge to kiss her that is so strong I'm afraid it might kill me if I don't.

'What am I going to wear if I see her tonight?' Suddenly, my jeans, shirt and cardigan don't seem nearly good enough in case she's still there. She made me feel so feminine, the chivalrous way she spoke to me, how she touched me and looked at me... It's been a long time since I dressed up for someone, and I liked it. Changing my mind, I decide that my job may not be my priority right now after all. *'Just for today.'*

"Jeff?" I say, turning to him with a smile. "Would you mind taking over my last appointment? I have to run to the pharmacy."

"Really?" Jeff frowns. "You trust me with Target?"

I hesitate for a moment, contemplating if I really want to leave the less experienced Jeff with my biggest client. It took me three years to get them on board and if he screws up there's no coming back from it. My insane need to be prepared for her is bigger than my ambition though, and so I nod and cast him a big smile.

"Yes, of course I do. You'll be great, trust me." Getting up from the table, I grab my purse and wink at him before walking out of the stand.

4

_____

As much as I hate to admit it, I'm disappointed that May, as she calls herself, is not here when I take a seat at the hotel bar in the very spot she was sitting yesterday. After showering and getting dressed up, I even managed to get here at the same time, just in case she had a regular schedule too. I should have guessed that she doesn't, though, because nothing about her pointed to anything scheduled.

It's busier today, and I'm silently hoping the stool next to me will stay free in case she sees me and decides to join anyway. Unfortunately, it's not May, but Jeff who comes rushing up to me. When I see his wide grin, I can't help but smile too, because I know it's got something to do with the client that he took over from me.

"Why are you so chirpy?" I ask, already knowing the answer.

"Why am I so chirpy?" Jeff repeats my question and shifts on the spot like an excited toddler. I love his enthusiasm and sometimes I wish I felt the same after fifteen years in the same business. I'm dedicated, sure. But Jeff still has the drive I used to have and I'm a little envious of him. "You're never going to believe this; we've just had a massive order on that new fabric you're presenting on Monday!"

"Already? That's fantastic, Jeff." Giving him a pat on his shoulder, I hold up my gin and tonic in a toast. "What are you drinking?"

"I'll have a beer. Could really do with one now." Then Jeff's gaze travels over me. "You look different. Why did you get changed?" He gives me an almost disapproving look as he glances at my hair. The braid he's used to seeing has been released into long, free flowing blonde locks and I'm pretty sure he's judging me for wearing a little makeup too.

"I needed a shower," I say in my most nonchalant tone, knowing he's confused about how I look. Clothes are generally not my priority and the only reason I brought the dress I wore last night was in case I got asked to go for a fancy dinner somewhere but so far, everyone seems quite happy staying at the hotel.

Instead of going to the pharmacy, I took a taxi to a department store and bought new lingerie, a dress, and the pair of black killer heels with red soles I'm wearing right now, but Jeff doesn't need to know that. The black dress is revealing in the sense that it's backless, but other than that it's decent enough to wear amongst my fellow vendors, who are mostly dressed in jeans, preppy shirts and cardigans. The shoes on the other hand, are a little more daring. They're high and elegantly heart-shaped at the toe, with stiletto heels, and they're so not me. I'm grateful for the bar, covering my thighs and feet because if Jeff saw my shoes too, he would seriously question what I was up to. I have no wicked plans for tonight, or so I tell myself, but if she shows up, I want to look good.

Jeff is not exactly a Casanova, and women have never

been his strong point. That's what makes our working relationship so great, though. Being together for twelve hours a day creates a bond, and the risk of him starting to see me in any other way than a friend is something I'm happy to do without because he's like a brother to me.

"I get that but..." Jeff pauses. "You've dressed up." Again, he gives me a baffled glance-over and his frown almost makes me believe I look disgusting beyond imagination. But I know I don't. In fact, I like the new me, even if it's only for one more night.

"Yeah, well, everyone wants to look nice now and then." The memory of her intense eyes flash before me, and a shiver runs down my spine. Every time my mind goes there, I clench my thighs together and have to force back a whimper. Her hands on me, her thrusts, her mouth claiming mine... I didn't mind going back to my own room. In fact, I needed some alone time to collect myself. After finally calming down, I had a long shower and it took me at least ten minutes to register the water was cold because I was so overwhelmed by what she'd done to me.

"I suppose so." Jeff picks up his beer and decides to let the subject slide, still refusing to give me a compliment of any kind. "Anyway, take a look at these numbers from today." He holds his phone out for me and takes a sip from his drink. His animated state makes me chuckle, and it is then that I feel a hand on my back. I freeze because I know it's her. Before my mind has had a chance to process it, my body is already reacting to her closeness. The flutters, the wetness, the ache... '*Jesus.*'

"Hi," I say, and smile as I turn to her, hoping I don't sound too keen.

"Hi." She sits down next to me and nods politely but other than that, doesn't acknowledge me. Instead, she asks the bartender for a Scotch as she rests her chin in the palm of her hand, looking a little bored. The barstools are placed close to each other and when she shifts, I feel her thigh against mine. I stare at her, completely taken aback by her lack of engagement and basic manners. It's rude, not to mention hurtful. I take a beat to process the fact that she's ignoring me and contemplate saying something that might shake her a little, although I doubt that's possible. I don't though. I never yell at people and now is not the time to start, I tell myself. Especially not with Jeff sitting next to me. No one here can find out what I got up to last night. My colleagues in the industry respect me, take me seriously and I'd like to keep it that way, so I turn away from her and face Jeff again.

"Are you okay?" he asks me. "There's something off about you today."

"Yeah, I'm fine, just a little tired." I lean in closer and try to concentrate on the numbers he's showing me when suddenly I feel a flirtatious hand on my knee. Immediately, I freeze again and try not to flinch. A fire spreads out from my core, numbing everything around me for a moment. The chatter, the light jazz music, the lights, even Jeff is forgotten. '*So this is what she wants,*' I think, when I realize this was her plan all along. I'm so aroused just from the touch of her warm hand that my brain shuts down. "Looks good," I stammer at Jeff, trying to sound like myself. Truth is, I have no idea what is on the screen because there is no way I can concentrate while her hand is on me.

"Looks good? Are you kidding me, Em? We're already thirty percent over target, this is going to be our best year ever. I thought at least you'd have something more to say than just 'looks good.'"

Her hand slides further up then, its progress so slow that

I can barely feel her teasing fingers move. The hem of my dress moves along with them, and I'm worried Jeff will notice if she doesn't stop soon. Even though I know he can't see what she's doing, I try to keep my composure, but I know the soft gasp that escapes my mouth is giving me away.

"I'm sorry," I mumble. "Of course I'm excited, but maybe we shouldn't be discussing this right now. I'd like to review it with fresh eyes." My voice sounds unusually high-pitched and it only gets more complicated when the barman asks me what I'm drinking. Thinking is extremely hard as I process his simple question. "I'll have another gin and tonic," I manage to say. "Cucumber instead of lemon, please." By now, I honestly couldn't care less what he throws in there but Jeff knows I'm particular about my small enjoyments in life and so I stick to my usual. My thighs are trembling as she slides her hand between them and asks for more ice in her own drink with the causal air of someone who's simply killing time. I can't help but turn her way to gauge her reaction. Her face carries no expression. If anything, she looks blasé, but when her eyes lock with mine for a split second, I can see a twinkle in them.

"Let's go through this tomorrow morning over breakfast," I hear myself say. I feel a little guilty for killing Jeff's enthusiasm, that would have been mine too if it wasn't for the fact that I'm fucking dying here. "I'm so tired that I can't even think straight."

One bold finger moves toward my pussy and presses against my clit. I gasp and take a sip of my drink in an attempt to hide the fact that I'm about to climax in a public space. 'This is not me.' Apparently, that's my new mantra, but I seem to be doing the opposite. Wanting the opposite. She pushes harder, moves her fingers lower, and makes slow circles with her thumb. It feels so good that I spread my legs a little, giving her better access to what I know will be a pair of very wet lace panties. I know she wants to know how wet I am and that turns me on even more. Only seconds later, when she pushes against my clit again, I feel a climax building. I panic at first, afraid I won't be able to hide it.

"Emily?" I hear Jeff call my name. He sounds worried but I'm unable to answer so instead, I lean over the bar and bury my face in my hands. Release washes over me and all I can do is give in to the moment while trying to keep quiet. It's not easy; I'm shaking, hoping my climax will stop but at the same time wishing it would last forever.

"Emily, are you crying?"

I try to get my act together and shake my head a little too frantically. "I'm fine," I say when I'm finally able to speak through ragged breaths again. I look up and manage a smile while I hide my trembling hands under the bar. "I'm really pleased, honestly. But it's been a long day and I think I need to stop drinking and head back to my room. I still have to prepare my presentation, so maybe it's better if we celebrate tomorrow." I wipe away the tear that's rolling down my cheek. I have no idea how it got there but I'll take it; it adds to the drama.

"Sure." Jeff puts his phone in his pocket and shoots me one more look, clearly still puzzled. "Let's go over it tomorrow. Meet you for breakfast?"

"Yeah. I'll see you at eight." I feel her hand retract so he won't see her arm there when he stands up and I wait until he's out of sight before I turn to her. "Who the fuck are you?"

"Are you okay?" She repeats Jeff's words with a mischievous smile on her face, ignoring my question. I don't even know how to answer that, so I say nothing. "Can I get you a drink, Emily?"

I shake my head, still lost for words, down the rest of my gin and tonic, and slam the glass down on the bar before reaching for the fresh one. "I still have one." She frustrates the hell out of me with her games, yet I can't seem to get enough of her. I don't do games and I don't have much experience on the adventurous front when it comes to sex either, but I do usually have sense, and nothing about what I've just done makes any sense to me at all. It's just not me. *'Keep telling yourself that,'* the voice in the back of my mind tells me.

"I'm going to order some Champagne anyway," she says matter-of-factly. "I'm sure you'll want some later, when you're exhausted and thirsty." Her eyes roam over me, from my face to my breasts, before stopping at my shapely legs. Then she moves back on her stool so she can see my heels. Licking her fingers suggestively, she gives me that killer smile again. "Not here, though. I'll take it to my room; I'll see you there in an hour." Producing a pile of cash from her pocket, she turns to the bartender and orders a bottle of Veuve Clicquot.

5

Once again, I find myself in suite 935. This time, I'm sitting on the couch, sipping the glass of Champagne that was waiting for me when I arrived. I'm still physically and mentally recovering from what she did to me at the bar, yet I'm also tense with anticipation and an overwhelming craving for more. It's hard to believe that I willingly went along with her game only an hour ago, right next to Jeff, who doesn't know anything other than that I was tired and having some kind of weird breakdown.

She's in the bathroom and I take the opportunity to look around for any clues as to why she's here, but there's nothing personal lying around, apart from an expensive looking navy blazer hanging over the back of the desk chair and a brown leather duffel bag next to the bed, zipped closed. Knowing there might be a wallet in the blazer pocket, or work files in the bag, I try to suppress the itch to investigate. 'Don't', I tell myself. I'm not someone who snoops around in people's personal belongings; I would never do that. 'The longer you sit here, the less time you have.' My eyes shift to the blazer again, and I almost jump up when the bathroom door swings open. She tilts her head and studies me intently and it makes me wonder if she has somehow read my mind and knew what I was about to do. I'm aware that I look guilty, just from considering doing something I shouldn't. I've never even gone as far as stealing a candy bar from the pantry when I was younger, and subconsciously, I reach for my necklace, then remember I took it off last night.

"Looking for this?" She grabs my necklace from her nightstand and hands it to me. Her hair is wet at the base of her forehead, like she's just splashed water over her face. The top three buttons of her formal white shirt are open now, and her sleeves are rolled up to just below the elbows. She looks softly butch and sexy, and when her lips pull into a small smile, I know I'll do anything she wants me to, no matter who she is or what's in that bag.

"You look really nice tonight, Emily. I like the dress and the heels. It makes me wonder what else you've got under there because I sense you've been shopping today." She sits down in the chair opposite me. Her posture is powerful; both arms on the armrests, her feet steady on the floor and her legs a little apart.

"I have," I say, still shaken with adrenaline. I fiddle with my necklace, then slip it into my purse. When she looks at the bottle on the table in between us, I pour her a glass and hand it to her. She doesn't thank me, and I don't expect her to. Taking a sip, she lets her eyes roam over me again, then settles her gaze on my heels. The fire I see in her eyes tells me she almost let her guard down for a split second. It also tells me she has a thing for high heels.

"Stand up," she says then, taking back control. Her casual tone makes me think she does this all the time, and I wonder how many women she's had in her thrall before me.

Hundreds? Does she do this every night? Pick someone who looks desperate enough to do what she wants because she gives so much satisfaction in return? I'm not sure of anything anymore but do as I'm told anyway, because how could I not? It's what I'm here for; I want to please her, simply because it excites me.

"Take off your dress. Leave the rest on."

My hands tremble as I pull down the side zipper, then slowly slide the dress over my hips and step out of it. I feel exposed but my confidence grows when she shifts in her chair, unable to hide her desire. I know she wants me and that's the greatest turn-on of all. Feeling wanted like this... I didn't know what it was like but now I thrive on it, need it.

The lace fabric of the black wireless bra I'm wearing is so thin that it's sheer and I know my hard nipples are clearly visible as I stand before her. My matching Brazilian hipster panties cover only a third of my ass, and the thought of having her hands on it soon makes me twitch.

"Come here." She pats her thigh and puts her glass down as I walk over, then straddle her lap. I hold my breath, aroused beyond control at being so close to her again. I shiver when her hands trace my heels, stroking them as if they're a fine art object. Then she rakes her hands along my legs and my hips before settling on my waist, and I wrap my arms around her neck as I lean in to kiss her. One of her hands moves into my hair, the other down to my ass, squeezing it hard while she pulls me closer and parts my lips with hers. Her tongue claims my mouth, and I moan into the kiss. *Fuck.* No one has ever kissed me so possessively before. No one has ever come close to what she does to me, how she makes me feel. It's crazy. She brushes her thumb over my nipple and when I gasp and arch my back, letting her know I need more, she yanks down one strap of my bra, exposing my left breast. Her hungry mouth closes over my hard nipple and it's deliciously warm and wet as her tongue circles around it, driving me wild. I cry out in surprise when she bites down on the spongy tip, just hard enough to hurt, and thrust my hips forward as my head falls back. She pulls my bra down entirely and turns her attention to my other breast, biting even harder this time. It hurts and as I'm balancing on that perfect edge of pain and pleasure I never knew existed, I never want her to stop.

"Fuck!" I scream and close my eyes.

"Do you like that?" She asks.

"Uhuh." I want to say more, encourage her to go on, but I'm silenced by another tug of her teeth. Riding her lap, I thrust into her as she feasts on me and I actually think I'm going to lose all sense of control. Her hand on my backside moves to the front, in between my spread thighs. She roughly pulls my panties to the side and, as if I know what's coming, I brace myself for the mind-blowing flash of delight that inevitably radiates into every part of my body when I feel her fingers running through my aroused folds. She lazily traces her fingers up and down, then settles on my clit, the sensation making me gasp in ecstasy.

"I love how wet you are," she hisses in my ear as she slides a finger inside me. "It feels so fucking good."

"Only for you," I whisper, and it's true. I lift my hips and gasp when she adds another. Lowering myself onto her fingers, I'm trembling all over as she fills me up and again, there's that smile that strikes me deep in my core.

"Good girl."

I shake my head at the irony of that statement because it's clear that I'm not as good as I thought I was. She moves with me as I ride her fingers, faster and deeper. When her teeth start tugging at my nipples again, I know I'm going to come harder than I ever have. Her arm around my back holds me up because my muscles are giving up on me now. A sharp stitch of pain, then wave after wave of euphoria wash over me as I clench around her dexterous fingers and tense up in her grip. The throaty sound that escapes me doesn't sound like me, but I don't even attempt to hold it in. It feels liberating to let it out, to release something that's been buried so deep for so long. I feel dizzy and realize I must remember to breathe. When I open my eyes and look at her, her fingers are still inside me and although I want them to stay there forever, she slowly retracts her hand. There's something in her gaze that looks pretty close to tenderness, but I tell myself it's just in my head. Still, I kiss her softly, and when I feel her hand cupping my cheek, I know I wasn't mistaken.

6

_____

"Tell me something about yourself." We're still in the same chair and I'm sitting on her lap, my legs flung over one arm and my elbows behind me resting on the other, when she asks the question that takes me by surprise. Her hand is in my hair, twirling my blonde locks around her fingers. It seems strange for her to want to know something personal about me, considering how private she is herself.

"Why?" I ask.

"Because I'm curious." She trails a finger down my neck and over my shoulder and the light touch makes the hairs on the back of my neck rise.

"I'm curious about you too." I tilt my head and lock my eyes with hers. "But that still won't get me anywhere, will it?"

"I know. I'm sorry I can't talk about myself, but you intrigue me, Emily, and so I'd like to know more about you. This perfectly controlled front you put on is such a contrast to how free you are with me. Sexually, I mean..." She pauses. "And I get a feeling that's new to you, which intrigues me even more."

"Sounds to me like you've figured me out all on your own," I say with a little sarcasm running through my voice. If she's not giving anything away, why should I?

She shrugs, amused by my reply. "I could try, if you want?"

"Fine. Try me." I lean back and wait for her to make her first mistake. She doesn't seem like a person who makes mistakes but I'm not exactly an open book and there's no way she can read me. My grandmother used to worry I was borderline psychopath when she was still alive, as I rarely show signs of emotion. Although I always dismissed her concerns, I still thought about it a lot over the years and have come to the conclusion that I'm simply a closed person, who only cares about a few things and people in life. If that makes me cold, then so be it. One thing is certain; I'm far from cold when I'm with her, and it's almost scary how she makes me feel like I'm on fire whenever she as much as looks at me.

"I'd say your upbringing was conservative, perhaps to the extreme. Religious?"

"Hmm..." I fall silent for a moment after her first guess is spot on. "Yes, it was. Both conservative and religious. But not in a bad way."

"Church on Sundays?"

"Yes."

"From a small town? Still close to your parents?"

"Yes. How could you possibly know?" She sounds so sure of herself that I'm starting to think she's done a background check on me.

"Your silver cross around your neck kind of gave you away when I met you at the bar, so the religious part was a given. You fiddled with it when you were nervous, and I could tell it was important to you, yet you didn't put it back on when I handed it to you earlier. You have no tattoos or signs of previous piercings, and although that is not a reliable factor to base assumptions on, my guess is that you weren't much of a rebel when you were younger. So, it makes sense that you've stayed close to your parents if they're still around. Want me to carry on?"

I'm so baffled by her observations that I don't know what to say, so I simply nod.

She gives me a triumphant smile, clearly pleased with herself, and carries on. "You were dressed fairly conservatively after the trade show, fitting in with the company you work for." She winks. "I looked them up. Although they might not be very exciting, they seem to be a good employer. I think your white, cotton shirt was made from fabric you develop and sell, and so it shows that you care a lot about your job and that you take pride in it. Right now, you look different though... You look like you're only just discovering yourself. As I said, you're fascinating."

She glances over my half-naked body. The straps of my bra have been pulled down, exposing my breasts but I'm still wearing my heels because they give me a sense of control. My hair is tousled and although I haven't looked in the mirror, I think I might have mascara stains under my eyes and the remains of smudged lipstick around my mouth.

"You're not wrong," I say. "What else?"

"You're confident, but that has more to do with your job and how comfortable you are in it. It comes across in your work environment. I can tell by your posture, how you carry yourself among your colleagues and how you interact with them. Outside, you're not quite sure who you are, though."

I nod again, realizing that she's right.

She pauses and glances at me before she continues. "You

feel no need to fill up silences with small talk. I like that about you, but what tells me more about you than anything, are your eyes."

My heart skips a beat when her gaze meets mine. "My eyes... What about them?"

"They hide nothing from me," she says. "And I like that. When I offered you a drink, I could tell straight away that you were a little guarded. Then I read curiosity in your expression and finally..." She smiles, bringing her mouth close to my ear. "So much desire that I just had to have you." Her warm breath sends a shiver down my spine.

"You seem to know me well for someone I met only yesterday."

"I believe I do." Her hand sensually caresses my thigh and I'm unable to suppress a soft moan. It's all it takes for my arousal to flare up again, to crave her like nothing else. "Your reaction to my touch is mesmerizing, I've never seen anything like it. You love that I'm in control."

"I do," I admit, and shift in her lap, allowing her hand to rise further. My voice catches as I ask the question that's been burning on my mind since we started this conversation. "How come you're so good at reading people? Or did you look me up?"

"I didn't look you up, just your company." She hesitates for a beat before she continues. "It's important for me to know who I can trust. In order to know, I need to read them."

"And why is it so important for you to trust everyone?" I ask.

She laughs. "Hey, don't change the subject. We're talking about you here."

"But you've made me even more curious now, it's not

fair." I run a teasing hand through her hair and kiss her. "So... you can read people and you're incredible in bed. What other talents do you have?"

She shakes her head and raises a brow. "Okay. I'll tell you one thing about myself, but it's all you're getting. I can do a bit of magic."

"Magic?" Despite her hand being so close to my panties now, the statement makes me laugh and I sit up. This woman is even more interesting than I anticipated. "Show me a trick then."

Of course, she expected my request and it doesn't throw her. It's like she's always one step ahead of me. "Sure." She reaches into her pocket and takes out a quarter. "Hold this for me."

I take the coin and study it, making sure it's real. My eyes are focused on it as there is no way in hell she's going to trick me from up close.

"Cover it with your other hand," she says. When I do, she folds her own hands over mine and shakes it.

I can feel it squashed between my palms, at least I think I do. She continues to shake my hands, and I laugh again, realizing how ridiculous we look right now. "Are we done yet? Or are you trying to distract me with whatever it is you're doing?" I still haven't taken my eyes from our joined hands.

"No, we can stop whenever you want. I just love listening to you laugh."

I hold still then, taken aback by her sweet words and when she removes her hands, I notice the coin has disappeared from my palms. A frown appears between my brows as I open her fists to check if she's holding onto it. They're empty, of course. "Where did it go?" I'm completely puzzled and very, very impressed.

She holds her hands up, making sure I know she's not cheating. "Spread your legs and you'll find it." Her tone is flirty and playful.

I roll my eyes at that because surely, I would have known if she'd put it there, however subtly. Suddenly, I feel something cold against my sensitive skin, and I do as she says anyway, only to find the coin when I reach down into my panties. "Jesus, you really are good at this. I can't stop laughing as I hold it up. It's covered in my juices, and that makes me laugh even harder.

"Thank you," she says, pulling me close to her.

"For what?"

"For laughing. I really do love the sound of it, it slays me." She looks at me earnestly. "For what it's worth, I think you're gorgeous and the sexiest woman I've ever encountered."

"No one has ever told me that before," I say, a blush creeping to my cheeks.

"Then whoever you've been with must have been crazy. Have you had many girlfriends?" The question indicates she's confident men are not my thing.

"Not many. Nothing long-term either. I tend to push them away when things get serious. I'm not sure why, I just lose interest."

She nods, as if she understands. "Have you ever been in love?"

"No," I admit, thinking this is quite an intimate question for someone who doesn't tend to get personal. Why she wants to talk now, I don't know, but she seems genuinely interested in me. "At least I don't think so. I would know, right? What about you?"

"I don't want to talk about me."

I sigh. "Well, then I think I'm done talking too."

"Very well." She unclips my bra and takes it off. If you're done talking, I can think of a few other things we can do."

7

I think she's under the shower. She didn't say anything before she went into the bathroom, but now I can hear the water running. Assuming she expects me to leave, I get out of bed. My legs feel like jelly after she fucked me for hours with her strap-on and with her extremely skilled fingers and tongue. I can feel where she's been as I walk and the worst thing is, I don't even feel used. In fact, I'm on a high and smiling as I finger comb my long, blonde hair that's turned into a knotted mess.

There's something protective about her, and I feel safe in her presence. Deep down, I know that idea is ridiculous and based on nothing, because I still don't even know her name but the mystery that surrounds her intrigues me rather than worries me. Besides, it's not like we're going to see each other again after I leave so why do I care who or what she is? The thought of not seeing her again makes me a little sad. I'll never be able to find her and, although I have no doubt that she could easily find me, I know she's not going to do that.

As I pick up my torn panties that she ripped off me right before we fell into bed, my eyes gravitate toward the leather duffel bag again. *'Don't do it.'* I'm sure there's a reason why she's so guarded, although her profound need for privacy seems to come with such secrecy, I find it hard to come up with a reason that doesn't involve criminal activities.

Intrigued to the point where I have to know now, I start analyzing the situation. I can't help it; I'm too curious by nature to let things slide. She doesn't seem like the kind of person to be on the ninth floor of a four-star hotel. Instead, she seems like a penthouse kind of woman, who would normally stay in a place much nicer than this. The Champagne she paid for in cash and the Scotch she drank earlier at the bar, not to mention her expensive shirt, tell me she can easily afford better accommodation than this. *'Is she trying to blend in? Why is she here? And why does she want to remain anonymous?'* I haven't seen her talk to anyone else at the bar, but then I've only seen her there twice and she was focused on me on both occasions.

I bite my lip, then glance over at the bathroom again before I tiptoe over to the bag and quietly unzip it. I find clothes, some toiletries and a notebook with some scribbles I don't understand. I check the inner side compartments but there is no wallet, and I can't find any travel documents either. My hand hits something hard as I reach underneath a pair of jeans and without seeing it, I instantly know what it is. Maybe I know because it makes sense. The way she behaves and never gives anything away... As I pull the gun out to take a closer look, the bathroom door swings open. She stands there and watches me, dressed in the hotel robe.

"What are you doing, Emily?" Her voice isn't accusing, simply curious.

"Ehm, nothing," I stammer, and throw the gun back in

the bag, immediately regretting doing so, because it might have been safer if I'd held onto it.

"Were you playing with my gun?" She locks her eyes with mine but looks calm and collected as she approaches me. There's not a single sign of panic in her expression and I wonder why.

"I was curious," I say, taking a step back as she comes closer. My heel hits the cold glass behind me, and I'm now backed up against the window. "About you. Why do you have a gun?"

"Why were you going through my bag?" She steadies the palm of one hand against the glass and leans in close until her mouth is almost on mine.

"Don't answer a question with a question." I hold my breath, thinking I should be afraid right now but strangely, I feel turned on instead. "It doesn't work like that. If you want me, you don't get to pull all the strings. You have to give me something in return, especially now that I know what's in your bag." My lips brush against hers as I whisper, and I can tell by the fire that flares up in her eyes that she likes that I'm not afraid.

She leans in with her body now, looking a little sad as she shrugs. "I'm sorry, but I can't tell you. It is what it is."

"What's your name?" I try to distract her with a different line of questioning, then kiss her softly. Of course, she doesn't answer, so I continue with the next question that's been burning on my mind. "Who the fuck travels with a gun and a strap-on? That seems like an odd combination to me."

She chuckles, clearly amused by that. "I like to be prepared," she simply answers.

"Prepared for what? To fuck a different woman every night?"

"Not every night. You're here again, aren't you?" She tilts

her head and looks at me intently. "I don't usually go back to the same woman twice, but I just couldn't stop thinking about you."

I manage to suppress an eye roll. "Why me?" I ask. "Seriously, why me? Am I supposed to be your alibi or something? Are you using me to get away with some hideous crime you've committed?"

"No." She takes a moment before she continues. "You had a certain sadness about you when I saw you at the bar last night. Not a deep sadness, just some kind of blankness to everything around you. I wanted to take it away, to make you feel something. That and..." She runs a hand through my hair. "I found you very attractive. I loved your voluminous hair and your lips looked like they were begging to be kissed so I couldn't resist."

"I don't believe you." I'm aware that I'm leaning back against the window with my full bodyweight, and that she's now leaning into me too. Her robe has fallen open and her breasts are warm and tight against me while the window is cold on my behind. Shifting nervously, I'm not sure if the intense tingle in my lower abdomen is caused by a fear of heights or a fear of giving into her again, because when she moves her thigh between my legs, that's exactly what I'm about to do. Her body feels so incredibly perfect against mine and I slide my hands into her robe and around her back, needing to feel her closer.

"Then don't believe me. Just enjoy the rest of the evening with me." She takes my hand and asks: "Are you joining me in the shower?"

Swallowing hard, I look at the door. Leaving now would be the wise thing to do, but I don't want to. If this is our last night together then I'll take whatever time she's willing to give me, gun or no gun. Knowing I'm probably making a huge mistake, I nod and let her lead me toward the bathroom.

8

―――――――

"I'm looking for my friend May in room 935," I say to the receptionist. "I was supposed to meet her, but she never showed up. Could you please tell me how long she'll be staying for?" I leave it at that. It's two am and I'm pretty sure the hotel staff don't care what people are up to, and at what time of the night, as long as they pay and tip. I waited for an hour until I came down here and I'm pretty sure she's sleeping now.

"May Ferguson. Yes, I have her here." The man picks up the phone and dials the room number.

"No." I wave a hand to stop him from what he's doing. "It's late so no need to call. I just wanted to know when she's checking out." He hangs up, then narrows his eyes as he clicks on the booking. "I apologize. She was a no-show, never checked in. We kept the room for her in case she showed up later, because she'd already paid up front, until Tuesday." He shoots me a regretful look. "I'm sorry, I can't help you any further I'm afraid. Are you worried?"

"No, not at all. She's a busy woman and she does this all the time. Thank you for checking." I give him a friendly smile. "I'm sure I'll manage to get hold of her tomorrow."

As I walk back to the elevators to return to my own room, I realize she's been able to get into her suite without a key card. Whoever she is, she's a pro, hiding in plain sight. It also hits me then that I'm the only one who knows she's staying here. What does she want from me? Apart from sex, of course, there's no doubt she wants that. The dark look of desire in her eyes when she made me come over and over a few hours ago is something I'll never, ever forget.

The word 'alibi' slips into my mind again and I wonder how I would really feel if she was using me for some ill-gotten gain, because honestly, I think I still would have been unable to resist her, even if I knew she was.

Then there was the shower afterward, which was almost sweet, and confused the hell out of me. Standing behind me, she washed my hair, then soaped my back before pressing her hips into my behind as she kissed my neck under the running water. The awareness as our slippery bodies made skin-on skin contact still makes me quiver when I think of it. Her hands reaching around me, stroking my breasts, my hips, my thighs... She let me back her up against the shower wall and greedily, I worked my way down her body, kissing and nipping at every inch of her skin, until I was on my knees before her, looking up. Never have I wanted to taste anyone as badly as I wanted to taste her. She certainly didn't mind when I put my hands on her hips and leaned in to lick her in long and teasing strokes before sucking her clit into my mouth, hard. I loved how she grabbed me by my hair and pulled me closer to her need, and the deep, throaty sounds she made when she reached orgasm were so sexy that I...

I wake up from my steamy thoughts when the elevator

pings and the doors open. Stepping inside, I stare at my reflection in the mirror against the back wall, hardly recognizing myself. My usual outfit, consisting of jeans, a cotton shirt and shiny leather loafers, has been replaced by my new backless little black dress and high heels. My hair is down, and I look tired but also extremely satisfied and even a little smug. I smile at myself, and wonder how the hell I went from being a woman no one would ever notice, a woman who always played it safe and put her work and reputation first at all times, to a woman who's just had wild, mind-blowing sex with a stranger two nights in a row. A stranger with a gun.

I'm not usually someone who makes heads turn; I dress way too plainly for that. Not that I ever notice anything around me because I'm either reading emails on my phone or I'm lost in my own thoughts thinking about whatever my latest project is. But tonight, I apparently radiate something because when the lift doors open halfway up and a young couple step in, the man is unable to keep his eyes off of me.

I look different now, I know that, but she noticed me yesterday when I came back from a long day at the trade show, looking very, very plain. How could she tell I was desperate to be touched before I knew it myself? That I needed her hands on me more than I ever needed anything?

Getting out on the eighth floor, I walk the long corridor toward my room. When I take my key card out of my purse to open it, I notice it's already ajar. Normally I'd be alarmed but something draws me inside, like I can feel her presence. If she can open her own room without a key, then mine shouldn't be a problem either. My pussy twitches and my heart beats faster just at the thought of her waiting there. How can she have such power over me? Make me ache for her after only two nights together? I let out a deep sigh of relief when I see her bag on the floor and smile when I spot her in the chair by the window.

"How did you get in?" I ask innocently, shuffling from one foot to the other.

"I think you know exactly how I got in." She raises a brow and looks amused, sitting back with one leg crossed over the other. "You've been checking up on me. Find anything interesting?"

"No." I shake my head. "Only that you never checked in and that your last name is Ferguson. Although I doubt that's your real name since you're sitting here now and have not only managed to get into your own room without a key card, but also into mine. How did you know what room I was in anyway?" I close the door behind me, walk over to her and step in between her legs as she uncrosses them.

"Well done, Sherlock." The sexual tension between us immediately flares up when she slides a hand up my leg. "Now I have a problem, though. They called the room and I'm not sure if it's safe to stay there anymore since you went snooping around." Her smile tells me she almost expected me to do what I did. "Don't worry," she adds when she sees me biting my lip. "It's okay, but now I have nowhere to sleep tonight. It's a big day tomorrow and I'm really, really tired. Can I stay here? Your room number is written on the packet containing your key card, by the way. You left it on the bar yesterday."

The surprise on my face must be obvious because for a split second, a flash of insecurity settles over her devilishly attractive features. I know she's not the sleepover type, but then I suppose I've messed up her original plan, whatever that was. There's no point asking because she'll never tell me. "You want to spend the night here?"

"Yeah, I do. Or what's left of the night, anyway. I'll find another place tomorrow."

"Okay," I say, trying not to sound too excited as I kick off my heels. "I'm here until Tuesday so you can stay tomorrow too, if you want."

Getting up from the chair, she grabs hold of the hem of my dress and slowly lifts it up, inch by inch. I know she likes that I'm not wearing any panties; I didn't bother to put them back on when I left her room because they were ripped, and they ended up in my purse instead. My bra seemed to be missing too so I gave up on looking for it. I shiver when I lift my arms as she pulls my dress over my head, revealing my naked body. She looks me up and down with intense hunger in her eyes, then shakes her head and composes herself. "As much as I want you right now, I'll let you sleep for a while. We both need it."

9

Her stirring beside wakes me up and I look at the clock on my nightstand. It's only four am and I'm grateful that I still have a couple of hours left before my alarm goes off. I'm exhausted, both mentally and physically, but when I close my eyes again, I miss her, so I turn to watch her sleep instead.

I want to hold her, but the intimacy of doing so scares me. I've never felt the need to hold someone in bed, and I've never liked my partners holding me either. Sometimes I've let them, just because it seemed like the right thing to do, but I always escaped from their arms as soon as they dozed off.

Physical affection was never part of my strict protestant upbringing, and although I know my parents loved me and wanted the best for me, I don't remember them ever giving me a kiss or a hug. Our household was run like a military base and being an only child, they were not only hugely protective of me, but also had extremely high expectations. Discipline, work ethic, manners and of course, God, were central to my life until I moved out but even then, I continued to get up at six every morning and made my bed like a well-trained soldier. I still eat my dinner at the kitchen table, never on the couch in front of the TV. Each day, I allow myself an hour of relaxation and do everything in moderation. Perhaps that's why I often come across as cold and standoffish when people first meet me, and I wonder why it was different with her, why I gave her all of me without even thinking. The overwhelming need to be close to her is a whole new sensation and although I'm hesitant, I still move over a little until I can feel her breath on my face and the heat radiating from her body.

She's dreaming. I can tell by how her eyelids flutter, and every now and then, she shakes a little. It feels wrong to watch her in such a vulnerable state, but I'm unable to look away. I like listening to her breathing. It's soothing and she seems so innocent now, not hiding behind control or whatever identity she's created for herself. What did she mean when she said that tomorrow was a big day? What is she up to? I can't imagine her killing someone but then again, I don't know her, so anything is possible.

I hold my breath when she mumbles something in her sleep and try to concentrate on what she's saying. I'm aware that it's intrusive, but I'm dying to find clues. It's hard to make out the words, apart from 'no', which she repeats several times before her voice grows louder. Her arms start to thrash, and I think she might be having a nightmare. Slowly, I reach out to wake her, stroking her shoulder.

"May, wake up." When she doesn't react, I move my hand to her cheek and speak a little louder. "May."

She gasps and sits up, breathing fast now. For a moment, she looks around the room as if she has no idea where she is. "Who is May?"

"You're May."

Knowing she's given herself away, she turns her gaze to me and rolls her eyes, shaking her head. "Fuck. Sorry if I woke you up. Nightmare."

"That's okay. Come here," I say. "You're shaking."

She rubs her temple, then hesitantly lays back down and inches closer. When I put my arm around her and pull her in, I can feel her starting to relax. I run my hand through her hair, cherishing the closeness and the warmth of her body. She likes it too; I can tell from the way she nudges her forehead against my hand and closes her eyes before giving a contented sigh.

"That feels great," she whispers, and wraps an arm around me in return.

I continue to stroke her face. "What did you dream about?"

"Nothing, I don't remember." Her gaze is vacant, and I know something is bothering her. I decide not to pry any further as the chance of her actually telling me is very small. Besides, I don't want her to relive whatever she's just dreamt about because it seems like she's extremely worried about something. Her lips meet mine in a soft and tender kiss. It's sweet and I'm sad, knowing this is not going to last because lying here with her feels so right that I could do it every day for the rest of my life.

10

"Emily."

"Yes?" My voice is sleepy as I blink against the ray of light that streams in through the gap in the curtains, then I moan when I feel her mouth on my neck. It's been a long time since I woke up with someone doing that to me, and it feels heavenly as I turn on my back to face her.

"Emily." She whispers my name again and I wish she would say it over and over because her voice sounds so incredibly sexy. "I need you to be awake for this, otherwise it wouldn't be right." I hear her chuckle at her own joke before her mouth moves down to my breasts, her tongue circling my nipples. Instinctively, I arch my back, pushing myself harder against her as my body responds with a feverish need. Her ministrations are having the desired effect, my nipples instantly responding to her touch, and it feels so good. Crazy good. My sleepy state only heightens the sensation of her warm mouth as memories of last night and earlier this morning slowly come back to me. The nightmare, holding her... I remember waking up a couple of times, content with feeling her arm around my waist.

She was holding me tight against her and as strange as it sounds, it felt comforting in a way that was entirely new to me. I'm not a cuddly person but feeling her breath against my neck and the heat of her skin against mine was so soothing that I didn't want the night to end. And now that her soft lips are trailing down my stomach, I certainly don't want the morning to end either, even though the sunlight tells me it's past seven already. My hands grab the sheets and I gasp when she spreads my legs apart, then lowers her mouth to my wetness. It's all she needs to do to make me squirm and cry out loudly in her grip. She holds my thighs apart as the licks between my lips, slow and sensual, up and down before she settles on my clit. When she sucks it into her mouth, my hips shoot up and an animalistic noise escapes me. I can't hold back any longer. I want it to last, but it's impossible with her tongue circling, then pushing down, putting pressure where I need it most. Explosive pleasure rushes through me as I grab her hair and push her tighter against my greedy pussy, bucking my hips against her face. She drinks me in, all of me as I lose every ounce of control I have left and cry out, shaking. I wonder how I've come from just waking up to the point of almost exploding.

My body is blissfully relaxed when I open my eyes a little later. Her mouth is still on me and heavy aftershocks take me by surprise when she dips her tongue inside me once again.

"Jesus."

She looks up and licks her lips, then gets up on her knees, looking like she's ready to do it all over again.

"Just give me a moment," I say, almost gasping when I see she's wearing her strap-on. This woman is insatiable, but then apparently, so am I if the past two nights are any indication. She has awoken a voracious appetite that I can't seem to satisfy and now I want her again.

She shakes her head as the corners of her mouth pull into a small smile. "Trust me. It's great to be fucked hard after you've just come. I promise." Slowly, she runs her hand down my waist and rests it on my hip. Her eyes turn darker and her smile fades then. "Turn around. I want you on your hands and knees."

I stare up at her, processing her demand, but she just tilts her head and keeps her expression neutral, although I can tell she's mildly amused by my reaction. Without thinking, I turn around and do as she says, shivering when she pushes her hips against my backside and runs a hand down my spine. I can feel the leather straps against my skin, the tip of the shaft against my pussy, making me ache with want and in an instant, my hesitation fades.

"Good girl," she says in a husky voice, and in that moment I know I want her to ravage me. I have no doubt she knows what she's talking about and my suspicions are confirmed when she starts sliding into me, little by little. My still oversensitive pussy clenches around the hard appendage and I push back against her, needing it, wanting more.

"See? Told you it was good."

I'm panting as she drives the shaft deeper, filling me up. The way she holds me by my waist, drives me crazy and I can't believe this is me, on this bed, in this room, naked on my hands and knees with this fascinating woman instead of getting up early to get some work done and practice my presentation. I have no idea what I'm going to say later, and I couldn't care less because it feels so good that I would scream her name if only I knew what it was.

She takes a firmer hold of my hips and moans as she

continues to thrust inside me, pulling my head back by my hair as she reaches the point of no return. Her breathing is heavy and so is mine when she starts fucking me hard until my arms and legs have trouble holding me up. Her hand reaches around me, and she brushes her thumb over my clit each time she thrusts, sending me to even greater heights. Another intense orgasm starts building, fading everything around me into a blur. I feel her jerking against me and know that she's about to come too.

I like it when she loses control. It means she's mine too, that I'm not just hers. She pulls me with her onto her lap as she sits back and throws her arm around me, continuing to stimulate me. Her other hand is on my breasts, squeezing my nipples hard as we climax together. It hurts but feels wonderful at the same time. The intense sound of her pleasure against my ear comes from so deep that I wish I could see her face right now, and she holds me so tight that I feel like we're one. I lift my hands behind me, rest the back of my head against her shoulder and run my fingers through her short hair, then lock them together behind her neck. My pussy is twitching around the dildo still buried deep inside me and when I turn my head against her neck, I can feel her vein pumping in the same rapid rhythm her heart is beating with mine. I don't want her to pull out of me and I don't want to let go of her. The fact that she doesn't let go either tells me she feels the same way and I allow myself to indulge in the moment for as long as she'll let me.

I don't know how long we sit there for, but I notice the light is getting brighter, and it must be late. A fleeting thought about my breakfast meeting with Jeff and my presentation comes and goes, but I shake it off and close my eyes until finally, she lets out a deep sigh.

"I have to go."

11

"I have to go." Regret rings through her voice as she says it again, this time dressed in jeans, a blue T-shirt and sneakers. It seems different to her usual style, but I suspect the aim is to blend in, wherever she'll be today. Or maybe this is the real her; I have no way of knowing. "If I don't see you again then..." She hesitates. "Well, it was really nice spending time with you. Thank you."

"Thank you?" I look at her and frown as I wrap myself in the hotel robe, not satisfied in the slightest with what she's telling me. Yesterday was different; I wouldn't have protested. Been disappointed, maybe, although I doubt it. But I would have seen it for what it was: just amazing, mind-blowing sex. This morning though, I can't seem to shake off the feeling that this is more than that, and I'm angry that's she's just leaving me like this. Our connection is deeper than we first imagined; I can feel it and I know she does too.

Soon, I'll be on stage in front of hundreds of people who will be wondering what the hell I'm talking about because I'm so unprepared that I won't make any sense at all. I've deserted my social duties, my sweet colleague Jeff, and all for a woman who's about to walk out of my life without even knowing how much she's messed it up. I'm fucked forever because I know that no one will ever compare to her. I may never see her again, but I know deep down that I won't forget her and now I'm even more pissed. Above all though, I just feel hurt and I shouldn't because I agreed to this, but nothing is ever that simple.

"So that's it?" I ask, an angry frown between my brows. "You're just going to leave? You're not even finally going to tell me your name or anything about yourself?"

"If everything goes according to plan, I'll be back tonight. But I can't promise you anything."

"Why? What are you going to do? And whatever it is, can't you get out of it?" I'm crying which seems odd, but I feel a sharp ache as I watch her sit down in the chair to tie her shoelaces. She really is leaving, and I always knew that would happen, but now that the time has come, I don't want her to go. I know it's ridiculous. I shouldn't be behaving like this, and I definitely shouldn't be crying over a stranger, but the sadness that fills me almost chokes me. "I don't want you to get hurt," I say, and I mean it. Because one thing is certain; whatever she's about to do, I know it isn't safe. It's not like she's going on a business trip, or meeting long-lost family, that much is clear. If she doesn't come back, I'll be forever wondering what happened to her, not even knowing if she's alive. All I'll know is that that over only two nights, she's made a lasting impact on my life.

"I won't get hurt. You don't need to worry about me." Her eyes meet mine and I can see that she is worried too, despite her attempt to reassure me.

"I don't believe you." I kneel down in between her legs and lock my eyes with hers. "I don't want to lose you, and I know this sounds weird, but I can feel there's something here between us."

"You don't know me, Emily." She sounds colder now, but I know it's only a trick to make this easier for me, or maybe even for herself. She wants me to be furious, to send her on her way. Still, her hand reaches for my face, and she wipes a tear from my cheek.

"You're right. I don't, and I never will." I shake my head. "Never mind, I'm making way more out of this than it is."

That remark seems to get to her because she leans in, takes my face in her hands and kisses me softly. "The people I'm doing this with... they'll never stop trying to track me down if I don't go through with it. I can't just pull out, it doesn't work like that." She smiles sadly. "This wasn't meant to happen. With you, I mean. It was only supposed to be one night while I was killing time in this shitty hotel. But you got to me somehow, and I'm very sorry if this sleepover changed things between us. As I said, you don't know me, and you probably wouldn't like me if you knew the real me."

"I'd like to decide that for myself," I say, my tone more distant now too. If she's trying to wind me up, she's succeeded. I feel pathetic when I continue, but still ask the question: "So you might be back tonight?"

"Maybe. I don't think it will make things easier, though. If this is hard now, then what about tomorrow?" Her hands run through my hair, tucking strands behind my ears.

"Then we'll deal with it tomorrow. At least I'll know you're alive." I pause. "So where are you going after tomorrow?"

"I don't know yet. I want to start living a normal life somewhere. Maybe on a farm in the countryside or maybe I'll blend into a city. I've always felt comfortable being anonymous." She bites her lip in regret, clearly thinking she's shared too much already. "This is the last time. It will all be over after today."

"Take me with you tomorrow," I hear myself say, knowing how crazy that sounds.

"I can't do that." The reply leaves her lips more like a question than an answer, and I can tell by the puzzled look in her eyes that she's completely baffled by what I've just proposed. It wouldn't surprise me if she thinks I'm losing it because even I am starting to wonder about that. "I don't want to get you in trouble and besides, why would you want that? You have everything you could wish for. A good job, a home, a decent life. You seem close to your colleague and I assume you have friends too…"

"I don't care about my life," I retort, raising my voice. "I might not know anything about you, but guess what? You don't know anything about me either so don't tell me I have everything I want." It's not a lie. Right now, all I want is her. I don't know how I'll feel tomorrow but I do know that I've been spending far too much time on the safe side of life. Working my ass off for someone else to cash in, watching movies in bed by myself until I fall asleep and spending way too much time in my car. Suddenly it all seems like a waste of time compared to how alive she makes me feel. Still, the little sense I have left is telling me to stop making a fool of myself, so I shake my head and look into her piercing blue eyes, trying my hardest to keep calm.

"You're right. I don't know what's wrong with me. Please forget I ever said that."

She nods, then stands up, grabs her leather duffel bag and turns to me before opening the door. "I'm sorry, I can't."

12

―――――――

"I can't do the presentation. I'm really not feeling well." Jeff sits across the table from me in the breakfast room and almost chokes on his scrambled eggs as I say it, after joining him forty minutes late.

"You can't be serious. Is it that bad? You've never bailed on anything in the ten years that I've worked with you, not even when you broke your right arm." He frowns. "I was impressed by how fast you learned to type with your left hand by the way."

Jeff knows me well. I've always been a loyal employee, and under any other circumstance I would have given the talk regardless of a dysfunctional arm or a heavy dose of the flu. But misery is a different thing entirely and I don't deal with it well.

"Yeah, it's bad. And for your information, I didn't call in sick once in the five years before you joined either so I think I deserve an out." I shrug, sit back and push my plate to the side as I try to come up with an excuse. "I think it might have been those bar snacks."

Jeff looks at me with suspicion. "I don't recall you eating

anything at all. Did you even have dinner? Wait..." He pauses. "You're not pregnant, are you?"

Despite my gloomy mood, that borders on desperation, I almost laugh at that. Me being pregnant right now is about as likely as Jeff being pregnant, but he doesn't know I'm gay, and so I simply shake my head. Why I haven't told him at some point in the years we've worked together is beyond me. When I first started out, I guess I felt like it was too personal to share my private life with colleagues. Growing up in a small, conservative town just outside Phoenix, where my parents still live, I was so used to keeping quiet about my sexuality that when I started my job and moved to the city I simply carried on doing so.

It took my parents a long time to get over the shock when I told them I was into women at the age of seventeen. Besides the fact that it clashed with everything they believed in, their dream of me getting married to a reliable, family man and having children one day, crumbled too. I was surprised when they finally came around and were able to look me in the eyes again, but being an only child, I suppose they didn't have much choice. They asked me to respectfully keep it quiet so the good people in our parish wouldn't find out and being the obedient daughter that I am, I did.

Until this day, they haven't stopped trying to set me up with men, occasionally even taking me by surprise during Sunday dinner after church. Sometimes I show up to find my parents' friends with their single son at the table, always seated next to me. It's embarrassing how little I've stood up for myself, and how closeted I've always been, despite my parents and a handful of people knowing.

The company I work for is sizeable, and our textiles might be exciting to some, but the location of our factory out in rural Arizona means that the board of directors and management are not always the most open-minded either. It seemed convenient after my graduation to take the intern job I was offered through a friend of my father, who was the sales manager there at the time. The short commute and the chance to work my way up excited me, but now I wish I'd been braver and moved away farther instead of having my parents plan out my future for me. With all the best intentions, they even paid the down-payment on my apartment for me back then. It meant that I could afford to live on my own and be independent, but I'm pretty sure the fact that the apartment was located so close to their house had something to do with it too. Looking back, I was never really independent, and I was never really free.

"Are you sure?" Jeff pulls me out of my thoughts, clearly feeling the need to double-check. "Because if you are pregnant, you know you can tell me, right?"

"Definitely not pregnant, Jeff. Just food poisoning or something. I feel feverish, nauseous."

"Okay, fine. I'll take care of it, then." Jeff doesn't seem too sure of himself as he says it. He's never been comfortable with public speaking and always leaves it to me because I don't have a problem with it. Until today. I almost choke up when he makes the offer because I know it will make him anxious. "I'll let Randy know."

"Fuck... Randy." I roll my eyes, remembering our boss will be here today. He's not going to like me cancelling but I really need a break. The knowledge that I won't have to stand before a crowd in the state I'm in fills me with relief and I don't know whether I'm going to break out into hysterical laughter or cry. Either way, it will happen any moment if I don't escape to my room soon. "Thank you," I say sincerely.

"I'll manage." Jeff gives me a wink. "Whatever it is, you know you can talk to me, right? You were acting weird last night, at the bar." It's clear that he doesn't buy my story that I'm sick and it makes perfect sense he thinks I was acting weird, considering I was trying to hide my orgasm right in front of him.

"I know," I say and give him a grateful smile as I get up from the table. "Thank you, again. I really appreciate it."

Retreating to my room, I take a couple of long, deep breaths as I get on the bed and bury myself under the covers. It still smells of her and that brings tears to my eyes. I scold myself for getting emotional over this illicit liaison. In theory, it's ridiculous that I'm experiencing a sense of loss over her, but I know that what I'm feeling is real. She makes me experience emotions like no one's ever made me feel before. Not even close.

I wonder what she's doing right now. Is she killing someone? Shamefully, I admit I might be able to forgive her for that as long as the victim is a really, really bad person, and I sigh at my own immoral thoughts. What's happened to me? I know right from wrong, I don't obsess over people, I don't fall madly in love, I don't get hurt, I don't surrender, and I certainly don't sit around waiting for someone to come back to me. I'm in control, always. As my thoughts come and go, I realize that none of those things apply to me anymore. The sheets are infused with the scent of sex and that saddens me even more. Staying here might not be the best idea after all, so I get up and grab my purse, then call a taxi to take me to Manhattan.

13

The luxurious dressing room in Barneys on Madison Avenue is spacious and comfortable, with big mirrors, and a small dressing table on which vanilla incense sticks are smoldering. A friendly sales assistant has hung the fragile garments I've chosen on the back of the door, and now I'm staring up at them, trying to decide which one to try on first. After a mani pedi and a bikini wax in the beauty department—something I rarely treat myself to—I went to the hairdresser for a wash and blowout. It's not like I've got much else to do today and hiding in here is safer than venturing the streets of New York, risking my boss Randy passing me in a taxi, or bumping into colleagues. Killing time is the best thing to do for now, and although it doesn't take my mind off of her, telling myself she'll be back tonight and acting accordingly is better than sulking in my room.

The first thing I reach for is a navy blue bra, edged with black lace over the balcony, and a pair of matching Brazilian panties. The material feels expensive and the thought of wearing this sexy lingerie for her excites me. My breasts are smaller than average, and unlike most lingerie, it fits me perfectly. As if it's meant to be, my body looks good in it, with just the right amount of skin covered to leave something to the imagination. I remove the clip from my hair and shake it loose, then turn around to check the back of the panties. My blonde, wavy hair covers the pretty straps of the bra. It's getting long now, and almost reaches my lower back. Since it's always been in a braid, I never thought of having regular haircuts and now I'm glad I haven't as it looks pretty sexy, hanging loose.

I face the mirror again and slowly slide a hand down my breasts and my stomach, and it's amazing how even my own touch makes me shiver today. She's switched me on sexually, turned my dial up so high that even the slightest sensation feels like lightning. How she did it, I don't know but she has me under some kind of spell and the sexual frustration I'm now experiencing following her departure is not subsiding in the slightest. I feel sore and my muscles are deliciously tired from last night and this morning. Taking a deep breath, I fight back an uncontrollable urge to release myself from the throbbing ache between my thighs, wondering if it will ever go away.

Feeling sensual and sexy is a new concept to me, one that I'm more than willing to embrace because I've needed it more than anything. After the past two nights, I crave sex like never before. I walk around thinking of it constantly, returning again and again to images of her consuming me, the flash-backs vivid and arousing, like they're trying to swallow me whole.

Conscious of the shop assistant waiting outside the dressing room, I compose myself, resisting the impulse to slide my fingers into the panties I haven't even paid for yet. At this point I try on the rest of the garments, just to give me something to do while I'm killing time. The black suspenders and sheer hold-ups—things I've never worn before—are a little tricky to handle at first, but once they're on, I know that I want her to see me like this. *La Perla* is clearly my brand and despite the hefty price tag, I decide to buy everything. It's the first rash decision I've made since accepting my last promotion on the spot two years ago, although that one doesn't really count as I'd been hoping to get it for months and so it wasn't exactly spontaneous. And now, here I am, head of sales at one the biggest textile companies in the US, buying seductive lingerie in the hope that my criminal lover will come back to me instead of delivering one of the most important presentations of my career.

Bailing on the talk doesn't bother me one bit because I've simply stopped caring all that much. How that changed overnight is a mystery to me, but I try not to overthink it. Apart from the first day, I've taken nothing in from this business trip and if I never close a deal again, I'm okay with that because there should be more to life than just work. I'm done with always doing what's expected of me, and for once, I want to be bad. Really bad.

"Are you alright in there?" the shop assistant asks, and I quickly strip myself of the lingerie before putting on my jeans and my white shirt.

"I'm fine, thank you. I'll be right out." After applying more of the bright red lipstick I've just bought, I nod into the mirror, telling myself that I am. Whether she comes back or not, something needs to change, and the lingerie is a good start. Then I hand all the delicate garments to the shop assistant, including a long, navy satin robe, and reach into my purse for my credit card.

14

'*She's not coming back,*' I think to myself as I look at the time on my phone again. It's past nine pm and the feeling of unease grows. I try not to worry about the fact that she may be hurt or even dead, but it proves impossible. After pacing for hours, I retreat to my bed and fall back against the pillows, wearing the satin robe and lingerie I bought earlier today while Jeff thought I was sick in bed. All for her, just in case she decided to come back.

It had given me a little hope; the shopping, preparing for our night ahead, wanting to be ready for when she knocked on my door. How did I become so desperate? How did I get so sucked up in her that nothing else seems to matter? Who am I? Have I lost myself or is this the real me? My emotions are all over the place and I wonder how I went through life feeling so numb for all those years. Was I happier last week, when I was comfortable, and everything was predictable and in order? Or was I simply existing, letting one day after another pass me by without feeling a thing? I've had happy moments, sure. The occasional party, times with my family or friends when we celebrated birthdays, holidays... but I have trouble coming up with anything memorable. One thing is certain though; I've had very few unhappy ones. There was little sadness in my life, and I don't remember the last time I cried, apart from this morning, over her.

Once again, I tell myself this is not me, but by now I know I'm only fooling myself. Still, despite worrying about her to the point that I'm almost losing the plot, I wouldn't have missed those nights for the world because they changed everything. In a good way or a bad way is still to be determined. My hope is declining with every second that passes, and those seconds have never gone by so slow. It's like I'm in a different dimension, where everything happens at a snail's pace and my brain is fogged by confusion as I'm desperately trying to hold onto something that's gone.

I turn on the news, looking for clues. I know that's wishful thinking because she doesn't seem like a person who would do something so bold and public that it would reach national television. As far as I can tell there has been a gang murder in New York, a serious traffic accident on the I-78 Interstate Highway, and a fire at a high school. Apart from that, the other news topics are either out of state or international. I jump up when there's a knock on my door and my pulse starts racing like a freight train. The disappointment on my face could not be more obvious when I open up to find Jeff in the corridor.

"Oh, hey," I say with little enthusiasm.

"Hey." His cheeks turn bright red as he glances down at my cleavage for a split second, then redirects his gaze to meet my eyes again. "I'm sorry. I should have known you were asleep."

"It's fine, I wasn't sleeping." I tie my robe tighter and open the door further, inviting him in. Distraction might be for the best right now. "How did the presentation go?"

"It was fine," Jeff says, walking into my room and scanning my bed as if he's expecting to see someone in there. Of course, there is no one here, and the bathroom door is wide open, showing the only other empty space in my room. When it's clear that I have nothing to hide, he continues: "I'm not going to lie, Randy wasn't happy to hear you weren't doing it, but I managed." A small smile plays around his lips and I can tell that he's proud of himself. "I think I did pretty well."

"Awesome." I open the minibar and scan the miniature bottles of wine and liquor. So far, I've managed not to drink, but I think this may be my breaking point. "I'm forever grateful. Do you want something to drink? To celebrate your first presentation?"

"Sure. I'll have a glass of wine if you don't mind." He sits down in the same chair May sat on this morning and crosses his legs in a similar manner. Everything reminds me of her, even Jeff, apparently.

I pour the wine and hand it to him. Although I was close, drinking alone is something I rarely do, and grateful for the excuse, I pour one for myself too. It's not like he believed my story anyway.

"Feeling better?" he enquires before he holds his glass up in a toast and takes a sip.

"Not really," I admit, sitting down in the other chair next to him. Having her walk in any minute is a risk with Jeff being here, but I have little hope she will.

"Do you want to talk about it?" Jeff shifts in his chair, perhaps uncomfortable being in my hotel room while I'm only wearing a robe. Not because he has alternative motives, but because we rarely socialize in private settings, and it doesn't get more private than this. "We've worked together for ten years," he says. "I consider you a friend, and if there's anything I can help you with, you need to tell me. Are you in some kind of trouble?"

"No, I'm not in trouble, but thank you for looking out for me. I consider you a friend too." I take a long drink of my wine, working up the courage to actually have a meaningful conversation with him, because he's right. After ten years, we really have become friends, and he deserves me opening up to him for once. *'It's time'*, I tell myself. *'No more hiding.'* "There's something I need you to know about me, Jeff. I'm gay." There. I said it.

I watch Jeff as his mouth gapes in a funny way. Just for a moment, it's taking my mind off of her, and I'm glad that he's here. I'm not per se nervous about coming out to him, but I can tell that he's surprised by what I've just said. Truth be told, I don't look gay in any way, if that's a thing at all. I look like your average girl next door, although today, with my hair blown out to perfection, my nails painted in a soft pink, and with my new ensemble on show, I probably look even straighter, and I can tell Jeff is confused.

"You?" he asks, as he leans forward and narrows his eyes.

"Yeah." I pause. "And I met someone here. A woman. The whole thing has messed me up pretty badly and that's why I couldn't do the presentation today. I'm very sorry for putting you in a difficult position, I know it was very unprofessional of me."

Jeff sits back, taking in what I've just said. "A woman, huh?" He looks like he has trouble believing it.

"Yes. But it doesn't matter. It's not going to work out." I let out a deep sigh. "The whole thing was silly and meaningless, but I got carried away and I shouldn't have made it your problem. I'm sorry." I know that's a lie but the truth will never leave my lips so I might as well shrug it off as a mistake.

"It's okay, you don't need to apologize." He pauses. "I'm so sorry to hear that. If she has such an effect on you, she must be pretty special."

"She is." I take another sip of my wine, thinking I should have had a glass earlier as its effect is already helping me relax. "But as I said, it's not going to work out, so I'll make sure I pull myself together. I'll apologize to Randy in the morning on our way to the airport." I'm actually surprised at how chilled Jeff is about my confession. He's surprised, sure. But other than that, he seems to be over it in a heartbeat.

He shoots me a sad look and shakes his head. "Fuck Randy. Some things are worth fighting for. Can't you take some vacation days? Stay here for a while longer? I've never seen you like this before, Em." He chuckles, pointing to my robe and my hair. "And I'm not just talking about your change of style, it's your whole demeanor, like your energy has shifted. I'll admit I was uncomfortable with it yesterday, because I've known you for so long and it was very out of character for you, but it all makes sense now. Don't you at least have her number?"

"No, I don't," I say. "And she doesn't want to be found. She captured me, heated the blood in my veins, then vanished. I'm still boiling and I don't even know her name."

Jeff's expression softens. "That sucks." He looks uncomfortable, and I check my robe in case it's fallen open again. It hasn't, and when I meet his eyes, I can see that he's truly agitated. "You know, we're the same, you and me. I should have known." Jeff's words are barely a whisper and I don't understand what he's trying to tell me until he spells it out. "I'm gay too." He avoids my gaze and focusses on his glass instead, which is almost empty now.

"You?" Our exchange is nothing short of extraordinary, and I think I need a moment to process his unexpected revelation. Jeff and I work closely, we've travelled extensively together, we've had after work drinks on many occasions, and never once did it occur to me that the wonderful man I've spent seventy percent of my time with, is gay. "How did I not know this?" I know it's a lame reply, but right now, I really can't think of anything else.

"I could say the same for you." Jeff downs the rest of his wine and stares at the door. I have a feeling he's not told many people in his life. Gauging from his reaction, I might even be the first so perhaps we're even more alike than he thinks. Suddenly he goes into flight-mode, stands up and says: "I should go."

"Wait." I take his hand as he's about to leave. "Thank you for trusting me and telling me."

"No. Thank you." He shoots me a tense smile before he squeezes my hand and walks out of the door. Once again, I'm on my own.

15

I hear the door open and within seconds, I'm out of bed. I must have fallen asleep because the alarm clock shows that it's one am. It's dark in the room but the shadow before me is unmistakably hers, and I let out a sigh of relief before I fall into her arms. After having given up all hope of ever seeing her again, holding her feels like coming home. She smells like she's just had a shower and her gray hoody is either freshly washed or brand-new. I don't know what state I expected her to come back in, if ever, but it certainly wasn't this.

"You're here," I whisper.

In return, she drops her backpack and puts her arms around me too, pulling me into a surprisingly intimate embrace as she inhales deep against my neck. "I'm here."

"Are you okay?" I mumble, taking a moment to really feel her before relaxing against her warm body.

"Yeah, I'm fine." I turn my head to kiss her, but she steps back then, as if it suddenly hits her that she's hugging me, and she switches on the light, breaking the spell. I don't beat myself up about it; it's not like I expected any different from her, but I still miss the contact.

As I look her over, I find myself scanning her for any traces of blood or bruises, but she's clean. Her short hair is brushed back from her face, resulting in a playful pompadour, and her blue eyes don't even look tired when she stares back at me. Is it relief I see in them? Hope? She looks happier than she did yesterday, and I can even see a twinkle in her gaze.

"I was so worried about you." I don't care if I sound dramatic. It's what I feel, and I have to say it. "I'm so glad you're back."

"Me too." She walks over to the mini bar, fixes herself a Scotch and holds up a second bottle for me.

I shake my head. My headache is only just starting to fade because I drank more wine after Jeff left. I sit down on the edge of the bed and watch her down the golden liquid in one swallow, before turning to me. Undressing me with her eyes, she rests her gaze on my cleavage where the top edge of my navy blue bra is visible. The hunger in her expression makes my breath catch. My physical reaction to her is so over-whelming that I wonder if it's normal. The nerves, the butter-flies, the all-consuming arousal, every nerve ending on high alert challenging my ability to think, speak, or even walk.

"You're still not going to tell me anything, are you?" I say.

"No, this is no time to talk. You've been stressed and so have I." She pauses and smiles. "We need to let off some steam and I happen to know just the right way to do that."

"Oh yeah? What's that?" I tilt my head curiously and look at her, her dimples weakening my resolve to try and get some information out of her. Although that's clearly not working, I still like where this is heading. The throbbing between my thighs is intense and every part of my body aches for her.

"You like to let go," she says. "It's the excitement of not knowing, the anticipation that gets you going." She picks up her backpack and zips it open.

"Not knowing makes me nervous," I disagree, although I won't deny that it's different with her. With her, the unknown is something I could explore forever.

"I know it makes you nervous, but you also thrive on it. You're used to being in charge of your life; planning, analyzing, always prepared for everything. You're a thinker, but sometimes it's nice to just let go, to surrender." She winks, then adds: "To me."

"Haven't I already surrendered enough?" I frown and watch her root through her bag before she pulls out four dark blue silk ties that match my lingerie perfectly. "If what I've done over the past two nights isn't surrendering, then I don't know what is."

"You have, to a point. But I want you to give up all control."

"Are you going to tie me up?" I ask, staring at the fabric as my breath quickens.

"Yes." Her short answer sends a rush of arousal through me. So simple, yet so powerful.

"I think I'm going to like that," I say, my voice a little unsteady. Do I like the idea of it? I didn't think I ever would, but seeing her fingering the strips of silk makes my pussy twitch.

"You will." She also takes out a blindfold, then changes her mind and tosses it behind her as she takes another step toward me. Now she's in between my knees, looking down at me, and she takes a wider stance, spreading my legs apart.

"We won't need that. I want to see your pleading eyes when you beg me to make you come."

I swallow hard and nod as I look up at her and in that moment, I know that I want nothing more.

"Do you trust me?" she asks.

"Yes," I whisper.

"I've never killed anyone." The random statement coming from her lips sounds like it's important, like it's something she needs me to know. "I've never hurt anyone either."

Again, I nod, and find myself to be far less relieved than I should be because right now, I simply don't care. "I believe you."

"Good." Leaning over me, she pulls at the belt of my robe and when it falls open, I see immense appreciation in her smile. She makes me feel desired, special, wanted, but that's only a small part of why I'm attracted to her. It's her energy that sucks me in. Her blue eyes have an intensity to them I've rarely seen, and she radiates calm and confidence like no one else. She's in control and I cannot begin to describe the excitement I feel at the thought of her tying me up and doing with me what she pleases. The sexual tension between us is explosive as I shift back up the bed until my head is on the pillows.

"Good girl," she says and crawls onto the bed too, then straddles me. The crotch of her jeans is pressing down on my pussy as she leans in and takes my wrists. I moan and lick my lips, longing for her to finally kiss me, because this morning seems like lightyears away and I really need to feel her mouth. Her face is close to mine and for a moment I think she will but instead, she gives me a teasing smile and starts tying my wrists together with such care and precision, that it tells me this is not the first time she's done this with a partner. I wiggle, instinctively trying to free myself, and when I realize I'm restrained, and completely at her mercy, my heartrate spikes. I lift my arms toward her, but she pushes them back.

"Did I say you could move them?" She shakes her head and arches a brow. "If you can't keep them there, I'll have to move you over to the side so I can tie you to the bedpost, but I prefer you in the middle with your arms above your head... it's very, very sexy."

"I'll keep still," I say, still wiggling a little as I try to get comfortable. It's a surprisingly scary sensation to be in this position, to surrender to someone else. It didn't seem like a big deal at first, but it is. The thrill of giving myself to her is bigger than the fear though, so I nod, confirming that I'll be good. "I can't free my hands."

"That's kind of the point." She gives me an earnest look, then asks: "Are you okay with that? I'll untie you right now if this is making you uncomfortable."

"No. I want this." I say it so softly, I'm not even sure if she can hear me but apparently the fire in my eyes is enough for her to move back and focus on my legs. She takes my ankle and runs a hand up to my thigh, stroking the lace edge of my hold-ups.

"Good. I love what you're wearing for me. It's very, very sexy."

The warm touch sends a flash of heat through my core, and when she moves my leg to the side and ties it to the bedpost, a pool of arousal settles between my thighs. I feel exposed already, even though I'm still wearing my lingerie, but I want her to continue. She then shifts my other leg, pulling my legs wide apart until I'm spread-eagled over the mattress. My legs are now bound to each corner of the bed and I gasp at the sensation, knowing that soon she'll be able to do whatever she wants with me. After giving a final tug at the knot securing my ankle, she gets off the bed and looks down on me. The robe I'm still wearing is open, and I know my heaving chest shows that I'm turned on beyond imagination.

Don't move," she jokes, then she heads into the bathroom.

16

I'm so worked up, overtaken by a mixture of arousal and frustration, that I have no idea what to do with myself as I hear the shower running. I'm soaking wet, my pussy aches and I desperately need her to touch me but she's in no rush, most likely enjoying the thought of me lying here, waiting for her. Her shower seems to take forever and when she finally comes out in a robe and walks around the bed, I let out a sigh of relief.

"Are you still okay?" she asks, as she trails a finger up the inside of my leg. She retracts her hand just before she reaches the edge of my panties and the sweet torture makes me groan in frustration.

"I need you," I say, lifting my hips, trying to chase her finger as it moves away.

"You'll have to be patient." She gets on the bed, in between my spread legs and looks me over. Her eyes flash a darker shade of blue and I know she's having trouble holding back, aroused at the thought of what she's planning to do to me. "You're so beautiful, Emily." Leaning forward, she steadies her hands above my head to take my wrists, dips down and runs her tongue over my upper lip. The warm, wet touch makes my skin tingle and I take in a quick breath. When I lift my head to kiss her, constricted by my restraints, she lifts hers too, inching away from me. Teasing.

"Kiss me," I say.

"Ask nicely." She brings her mouth close to mine once more and by now I'll do anything just to feel her lips on mine. Anything.

"Please kiss me." I try to move down, knowing her knee is almost against my center, but she's holding my wrists and I can't stretch myself any further. The more I resist, the tighter she holds me, and I have no choice but to give up and patiently wait for her to reward me. Sensing my desperation, she finally brushes my mouth with her own, and after so long without feeling her kiss, I almost come from that alone. A muffled moan escapes me as I part my lips, allowing her tongue to claim my mouth with the most sensual urgency and need. She moans too, losing herself for what seems like minutes in a slow and incredibly sexy make out session, before she regains control and pulls out of the kiss.

"Fuck, I love kissing you," she says, sitting back between my legs again. Her gaze wanders south over my body, down to my panties. "Are you wet?"

"I'm so wet," I say, bucking my hips. "I..." When her hand moves in between my legs and strokes my swollen and oversensitive lips through the thin lace, I'm so close to climaxing that I can't even speak.

"My God, you are." She backs away again, and I feel like shouting at her to take me. "Now... what am I going to do with you?"

"Anything. Everything." I'm panting before her as she opens my robe further, then reaches under me and unhooks my bra. She pushes it up over my breasts and sucks a nipple into her mouth. I know she likes my nipples; the way they're always hard for her, instantly reactive and so sensitive. When she bites down, a flash of pain shoots through me but it feels so good that I push against her. She lets go when I gasp, then turns her attention to my other breast while her hands travel down my waist. Her fingers are spread wide, her pressure hard, and I can feel the need in her touch. She's trying to hold back because she wants this to last. Her mouth covers my ribcage and my belly before she reaches the lace edge of my panties. Slowly, she runs a finger over it, then underneath, barely skimming the small strip of hair. I ache for her to take them off but she won't be able to do that with my legs tied up. A smile appears on her face and her eyes twinkle as she tilts her head, clearly thinking the same.

"I'm afraid this beautiful, delicate garment will have to be destroyed," she says in a low voice before she takes hold of the thinnest part of my new, expensive, *La Perla* panties and rips them all the way through. She licks her lips as she moves the fabric to the side, then slides what's left of my panties down one leg until it reaches my hold-ups, attached to the suspenders, and stares down at my glistening wetness. The unconscious gesture is so sexy that my breath hitches as I watch her take me in. Her eyes are as dark as her thoughts, I imagine, and I can almost hear her mind churning, deciding what she wants to do to me. Her finger hooks under the elastic band of my suspenders and she lets it snap back against my skin. "These can stay on. I like them."

I've never felt so exposed and vulnerable as I do now, near-naked and tied to a bed, but I also know I've never been so turned on, and I hold my breath as she takes hold of my hips and bends forward to taste me. As soon as her tongue traces my lips, I cry out and when an orgasm threatens to take over, I buckle and instinctively raise my tied hands reaching for her hair. Immediately, I regret my mistake because she stops and sits up, then crawls over me to put my hands back over my head.

"I told you not to move." She casts me a teasing look. "Now I will have to punish you."

"I'm sorry. But you drive me wild. I can't think straight."

"Good." She seems pleased with my excuse, but still gets up to pour herself another drink, then moves one of the chairs next to the bed and sits down to watch me.

"Please," I beg. "Don't stop. I'm dying here."

She doesn't answer but instead, takes a small sip of her drink while she looks me up and down. I can tell she likes me like this; craving her like nothing else. After a couple of very long minutes, she gets up and moves back onto the bed. My pussy lips are swollen and overly sensitive, my clit throbbing with anticipation.

"Ask nicely and keep your hands where they are," she says with a hint of amusement at seeing the relief on my face.

"Please, please, can I come?" The words come out of me in quick breaths.

She nods and leans between my legs again. "Yes, you may." Slowly, she repeats the action that almost sent me through the roof ten minutes ago. Her tongue on me is heaven and the contact causes an even greater climax to build, drawing a loud groan from my mouth. My legs tug at the restraints, but of course, the ties don't budge and all I can do is surrender to the intense pleasure as she presses her full mouth against me now and does something incredible with her tongue that prolongs my orgasm, drawing a long and throaty cry from deep within me. It's fucking amazing and she doesn't stop until every aftershock has subsided and I'm completely spent. She looks up after I finally come back to my senses, and I can see that my reaction has pleased her. Dizzy and on a euphoric high, I meet her eyes and almost melt when they appear to see right into my soul. Our eye-contact has been intense from the moment we met, but now, it's not just lust anymore that passes between us. It's like she knows me and, however absurd, I feel I know her too.

"How did you do that?"

"It's easy. You needed that." She gives me a wicked smile, crawls up and brings her mouth to my ear. "But I'm not done with you yet. That was just to take the edge off." Her words make me quiver and my body agrees with her when she opens her robe and lowers her naked body onto mine. It feels amazing, warm, exciting and so sensual. I want to touch her, feel how wet she is, pleasure her, devour her, but I can't. As if reading my mind, she says: "Later." Then, her tongue claims my mouth and she grinds into my center. "I'm going to fuck you until you have no energy left. I want you to feel I've been inside you."

"Jesus," I mutter, before I'm silenced by another long and feverish kiss. She moves to my neck and I turn my head to the side as she sucks at my flesh. There will be bruises there tomorrow, but I don't care. She's marking me, branding me as her own and that's exactly what I want to be. Hers. The force of her hips driving into mine makes me burn with want and the submissive state I'm in heightens all sensations. She moves her hand down my body and in between my shaking legs. Instinctively, I want to close them, only because I'm tied up, but without warning she enters me, and I whimper in delight when two of her fingers fill me up. My pussy is clenching around them, pulling her in deeper, and I can barely breathe I'm so aroused again. She closes her eyes, letting out a sigh as if she's been dying to be inside me. I marvel at her face as she sucks in a breath. It's a beautiful sight, one that feels oddly private. Sweat is pearling on her forehead and I'm sweating too. Our bodies are overheated, blazing, raging with desire and I think I might spontaneously combust if she continues like this.

"You like that?" she asks, retracting her fingers.

"God, yes," I whisper. "Don't stop." Every nerve in my body is screaming out for her and the frustration of not being able to grab hold of her builds. My clit is so sensitive that I almost scream when she brushes her fingers over it.

"Ask nicely." She clearly loves to hear me beg, but I can also see from her expression she wants nothing more than to make me come.

"Please don't stop," I plead. "Please."

"Good girl." She plunges into me again, and this time, shifts her weight to my thigh, coating me with her own wetness. The sensation of it shatters me, causing intense pulsations to rip through me and I let out a strangled cry as she starts fucking me. Her hips move in the rhythm of her hand, faster and faster. Her other hand is in my hair, pulling my head back so our eyes meet. The ragged breathing against my mouth, the frown between her brows and her teeth resting on her delicious, glistening under lip tells me she's close too. I want to wait for her, but she's determined in her passionate quest to elate me. Wave after wave of delicious tension starts building up and I'm unable to hold back. Shifting her attention to my neck, she sucks my delicate flesh hard the very moment I burst and only seconds later, she climaxes too with a loud 'fuck' spilling out of her as she crumples on the bed. The primal growl of her voice echoes through the room, merging with my moans when she repeats the word over and over. I feel close to her, so close that my eyes fill with tears when she rests her head on my shoulder and takes me into her arms. The embrace is all-encompassing, tender, tight, honest, and I'm unfamiliar with passion like this. My previous lovers were only ever there for convenience, and although the sex was sometimes good, they never made me feel like I was at one with them. As her breathing steadies I know she will become distant again and I want to be inside her mind so badly it hurts.

"Untie me," I say. "I want to hold you."

17

My alarm goes off as I'm lying in her arms, kissing her after hours of passionate, steamy sex, then tender lovemaking. We're like teenagers, unable to keep our hands off each other and even though she's fighting it, I can see that she's slowly letting her guard down in the way she looks at me when I touch her and the way she keeps pulling me in as if she too, is dreading saying goodbye. Quickly, I turn off the noise that cuts through our dreamy euphoric haze like a sharp knife. I hate the loud beep and want to throw my phone across the room or even through the window. It's the sound of goodbye, the sound of the end of this wonderful thing we have going on. Jeff, Randy and I are leaving for the airport in two hours and I don't want to go.

"Fuck," I say, because I truly am fucked. There's nowhere to go from here and I wonder how long I'll be stuck in the memory of her. Months? Years? Will I ever be able to move on? To form relationships after knowing what it's like to be with her? So perfectly perfect, exciting, thrilling, beautiful, inspiring and life-changing... My fingers graze her breast as I put my head back on her chest. I see goose bumps appear on her skin and her nipple hardens. She lets out a deep sigh as I trace lazy circles around it, then trail my finger down to her stomach where I rest my hand on her soft skin.

"I know." She swallows hard, then says: "I trust you." Before I can enquire as to the meaning behind this random statement, she continues, lowering her voice as if talking to herself. "At first, I just did it for the thrill. I've worked for my father's security company since I finished high school and took over when he passed away. A couple of years ago I sold the business when it started to lose money." She pauses. "I'm an expert on security systems and can get into most buildings or systems undetected. I can erase recorded digital footage and replace it with an alternative image that is so precise no one would ever notice it's not real. Opening doors is like riding a bike to me, and even opening digitally controlled doors or safes is not that hard with the right equipment and research. It's a unique skill and one that's highly sought-after, but as you can imagine, it rarely involves a good cause and honest, decent employers."

"That's how you got into my room." I take a moment to process what she's telling me. So she *is* a criminal. Do I mind? The shock from her suddenly opening up to me seems like a bigger deal than the actual revelation itself. Carefully considering how I feel about this, I come to the conclusion that I'm actually relieved, because it could have been a lot worse.

"These hotel doors are nothing." She smiles and relaxes a little when it's clear that I'm not going to jump out of bed and run for the hills. "And just so you know, I don't make a habit of letting myself into people's rooms or homes, and I never steal anything either. Well, not personally anyway. But the people I work with do steal, and they pay me for my services."

"How long have you been doing this?" I ask.

"The breaking and entering since I was about eighteen. The side job I've been doing for twenty years. I'm forty-seven now and retiring. Yesterday was my last gig."

After doing the math, I conclude that she's twelve years older than me. I'm surprised at this, because she comes across as younger, but perhaps her unconventional lifestyle has something to do with that.

"Did your father teach you what you know?" I ask. Suddenly, there doesn't seem nearly enough time left. Now that she's finally talking, I want to know more. I want to know everything.

"He taught me the basics, but it was entirely innocent. My father was an honest man; he would turn in his grave if he knew what I'd been up to. When he first started his business, and people in our little town had locked themselves out, he used to send me over. It was much easier to pick locks instead of replacing them, and in the end, it was cheaper for the customer too. Everyone in the small community knew about my skill but they also trusted me not to abuse it. I was a good kid when I was younger, never any trouble at all."

"What about your mother?" I ask.

"I never knew her. She left shortly after she had me. Postpartum depression. My father always expected her to come back, but she never did."

"I'm sorry about that."

She gives me a sad smile. "Don't be. I had a great childhood and my father was always my rock. I hate that I ended up doing the exact opposite of what he wanted for me. He died of cancer when I was twenty-six, just before I started getting involved with the wrong people.

Before that, he'd expanded into security systems of all

kinds, and I knew everything about those too. I studied them, learned about system hacking in my spare time and started testing my knowledge in bigger cities, usually telling my father I was going away with friends for the weekend. It felt like a challenge to see what buildings I could enter undetected, and there's something incredibly peaceful about dark, deserted offices and government buildings in the middle of the night. As I said, I never stole anything, just hung around. Sometimes I'd drink a beer on the roof to celebrate my secret victory. I set myself higher and higher challenges, thinking no one knew what I was up to but apparently someone had been keeping an eye on me and one day, I got recruited. I still don't know his name or anything about him, but it seemed incredibly exciting back then to be part of something so big and super-secret. My conditions were that I would only ever do jobs after hours, when no members of the public were present, and that I'd only break into big corporations, nothing small or private."

She takes a moment and I notice she has a faraway look in her eyes as if thinking back, with regret perhaps. "My first job paid incredibly well and soon I got addicted to both the thrill and the money. It was stupid, of course, and I know better now. Getting sucked in was inevitable, and it wasn't like I could just hand in my resignation. It's a miracle no one ever got seriously injured or died, apart from an incident when a security guard got shot in the arm when he pulled his gun on one of my team members. That was the only mistake we ever made; we thought he'd left for the night. Turned out he forgot something on his way out, then came back and heard us. I couldn't sleep for weeks after that, and I told them I wanted out, but by then leaving wasn't an option anymore."

"They wouldn't let you?"

"No, not until now." She pulls me in closer and places a soft kiss on my temple. "I asked after every single job, but they always said no. I guess it took time for them to trust me and to know they had nothing to worry about. But still... that gun in my bag is for my own protection. I still can't be sure that they might change their minds, and so I need to lay low, move around for a while until I'm certain they won't come after me. If nothing out of the ordinary has happened in three months' time, I can live under the assumption that I'm okay."

"I don't like that," I say. "I don't want anything to happen to you."

"I'll be fine. I can take care of myself." Her attempt to put me at ease doesn't work but I understand that she has no choice.

"Take me with you," I try again. It still sounds crazy, even now that she's holding me like she never wants to let me go, but I can't bear the thought of her leaving me, especially now that I've seen a snapshot of her true self. After everything she's told me I still want her, and the idea of going back to work in Phoenix and continuing my life as if nothing has happened this week seems unimaginable.

"You know I can't do that."

Her fingers combing through my hair brings a lump to my throat. "Will I ever see you again?"

"I hope so. But for now, I need to stay away from you so at least I'll know you're safe." She runs a hand down my cheek. "I'll come and find you when the coast is clear."

"Promise?" I sigh, a little more at ease knowing this may not be our final goodbye. Having her say those words is more than I could have hoped for.

She nods and gives me a sad smile. "I promise I'll do everything I can."

18

"Bye," I say, emotion ringing through my voice.

"Bye." She turns and lingers in the doorway. "Wait. I almost forgot the most important thing. "Blake. My name is Blake." She bites her lip anxiously. "I haven't said my own name in almost twenty years, I've always used an alias. I forgot what it sounded like."

"Blake," I repeat in a whisper, as if it's the holy grail, and I see her flinch at the sound of it. How lonely it must be to not have anyone say your name for so long, to live anonymously without anyone really knowing you. I suddenly understand why she is the way she is. Why she keeps her distance at all times, making sure not to come too close to anyone. She had no choice. "It's a nice name. It suits you."

"Thank you. I like how you say it." Blake takes my hand and kisses the back of it, then casts me a regretful glance before she walks away. "Bye Emily. I'll see you soon."

My eyes fill with tears as she disappears around the corner, and I'm hoping she'll change her mind and come back, but she doesn't. When I hear the ping of the elevator, I crumble down in the doorway. Hugging my knees, I finally allow myself to cry. I cry because I miss her so much already that it feels like a part of my soul has been ripped out of me. I cry because I can almost hear the emptiness she leaves behind and because I know her scent still lingers on my pillow. Panic chokes me when I weigh the unsettling possibility that this might have been the last time either of us will ever see each other again. That this really might be our final goodbye. My stomach hurts, I feel nauseous and my chest tightens to the point where I can barely breathe. I'm sweating profusely and my heart is racing at the thought of her getting into a cab and driving away from me, the distance growing until we're not even in the same time zone anymore. I wonder where she's going. Mexico? A Pacific island? And who is May Ferguson? Did she steal her identity? Suddenly, I have even more questions than answers and I curse myself for not asking them while I had the chance. I don't for one minute believe she would have revealed her plans, but her real identity, maybe? Does she have multiple identities? When I realize I might never find out, more tears stream down my face. A woman passes me in the corridor and asks me if I'm okay. I simply nod, letting her know I don't need any help or reassurance. Nothing can comfort me right now, but I still need to pull myself together before meeting with Jeff and Randy.

Crying is not something I do. I'm always composed, always in control over my emotions, and I rarely get upset. My parents always taught me there was nothing to cry over as long as there wasn't death involved. To keep my head screwed on and to not get carried away. Church taught me the same; to lead with my faith instead of my feelings, because that's how sins manifest. I haven't been particularly religious since I moved out of my family home, but somehow that teaching always stuck.

'Fuck that,' I think, because over the course of this week, I have committed more sins than I ever have during my entire lifetime, yet no one has ever managed to capture my heart like she has. She got me, whether I wanted her to or not, and I have no free will anymore. I'm all hers. She owns my body, my soul, my mind, and so it's okay if I cry. Maybe I need to let it all out right now, because I won't be able to talk to anyone about it. People will think I'm nuts if I tell them I have big feelings for someone I barely know. No one will understand, and I still find it hard to wrap my own mind around it.

How did she do it? How did she gain my trust from the start, even after I found a gun in her bag? And how did she manage to discover everything about me without revealing anything about herself until the very last minute? I know deep down, that if she'd let me come with her, I would have followed her anywhere. Across oceans, thought deserts, hell, even to another planet. I would have given up everything I've worked so hard for, and everything I love, just to be with her. My job, my family, my friends, my home... And all because I let her see into my soul. Looking back, I think I wanted her to possess me from the moment we met, like I knew she was the one.

19

"Anything I can do for you?" Jeff whispers as we pass Times Square. He gives my hand a squeeze, a sweet gesture of trust and companionship. After our conversation, I feel incredibly lucky to have him, and I squeeze him back and shake my head, trying not to cry with Randy in the front seat next to the taxi driver. Today, I hate the guy more than ever and I'm not sure why. His blotchy neck is hanging over the collar of his oatmeal colored shirt which looks like it's choking him, and I can see beads of sweat dripping down onto it, causing the fabric to go a shade darker. He's been blanking me since we met in the lobby this morning and I'm grateful for not having to speak to him.

"Thank you. But I'm okay." I fiddle with the silk ties around my neck, the same ones she used to tie me up with last night. I noticed my neck was covered in purple hickeys when I got ready to leave, and although I know this is a strange fashion statement, it's better than having them on display.

As I look out of the window and Manhattan passes me by, I feel immensely shielded from life and I'm suddenly overcome with an urge to be an active part of it. I love New York; it excites me. When I was in my twenties, I used to come here regularly on vacation and on the weekends, but over the past ten years I've done nothing but work non-stop. I wonder now what happened to me. Somewhere along the way, my life became boring, predictable and void of any passion or excitement. I know I did it to myself; I chose to hide behind a pile of work that became my security blanket. For no reason other than that it was comfortable, I pulled it up so high that no one noticed me... Until this week. I was sleeping and she woke me up.

"She's fine," Randy says, his first words directed toward me in a week. "Aren't you, Emily?" The sound of his self-satisfied voice makes me hate him even more.

"Sure," I answer absently, staring out at the city. It's breathing an energy that makes me long to jump out of the car and leave everything behind. I should have moved away from Arizona when I was younger. I should have gone back to university, to study art history like I always dreamed of, instead of settling for something safe. If I had, I could have been anywhere by now. Rome, Paris, Barcelona, here... I should have enjoyed life more, travelled more, partied more. I should have come out to my co-workers and everyone else around me, but most of all, I should have taken risks. Why didn't I? So many regrets run through my mind, as if a floodgate has been opened. I feel like I'm drowning at the thought of settling back into my old life and when I think of her again, I miss her so much that I feel physically sick.

"What was up with you anyway?" Randy barks then, as if he's been holding in his annoyance for hours, waiting to voice his opinion until he's about to burst. "You're always so well prepared."

"I wasn't feeling well."

"You've never let me down before." He grunts when the traffic slows down. "What the hell is wrong with this city?"

I ignore his remark, then say: "I'm tired. I need a vacation."

"That's not an option I'm afraid. We're very busy at the moment so you're going to have to pull yourself together."

A rage starts to build inside me, and I ball my hands into fists. Although my nails are digging into my skin, I manage to stay calm. "I've only taken ten days off in the past fifteen years I've worked for you, and none in the past three." I try not to raise my voice. "So yes, I do think I deserve a vacation. The situation is never going to change; it will always be busy."

Randy turns and looks at me as if I've lost my mind. "This is not a smart move, Emily. I thought you wanted that promotion to sales director."

Randy can shove the promotion up his ass for all I care, but I decide not to reply then, because I need her to be able to find me. She doesn't know anything about me apart from where I work, and although I have no doubt she's resourceful, I don't want to risk it. Jeff places a hand on mine, and I shoot him a small smile, letting him know not to worry about me.

There's suddenly a commotion in front of us and the taxi comes to an abrupt halt. Cops are everywhere, and hazards are blocking the road. It looks like there's just been an incident as road traffic workers are still busy blocking off the road. The car in front of us is standing still and our driver is unable to back up due to the queue that's formed behind us.

"Looks serious. This might take a while," he mutters. We all look outside, trying to figure out what's going on.

"Damn it, we're going to miss our flight," Randy hisses at the poor taxi driver, who has no control over the situation, then casts a shifty look out of the window. We're completely stuck now, and a cop gestures for us to stay in the car.

I roll down the window and hear onlookers talking as they try to catch a glimpse of the building that is heaving with officers and a bomb squad. It's a bank I notice as the crowd shifts to the side when barriers are moved farther away from the entrance.

"Do you guys know what's going on?" I ask the two skateboarders who are filming the scene next to our taxi.

"Not sure," one of them says. "But the bank just opened and then the cops showed up, so I guess it doesn't take a rocket scientist to figure out there's been a robbery."

My heart starts racing and I scan the area for ambulances, but I'm relieved to see none. Could this be what she was up to last night? It's unlikely. If this was her, then why didn't she disappear out of state before the bank opened? Why did she take such a huge risk by coming back to the hotel? Back to me? The only reason I can think of is too hard to entertain because it would mean that she really does have feelings for me too, and I let her walk away. I still smile to myself because, as much as that thought hurts, it also gives me the silent hope that maybe she really will come back to me.

20

"Em?" Jeff sounds excited when he calls me the day after we've returned from New York. We both have a day off as we've worked over the weekend and I've spent most of my free time in bed, digging through hundreds of May Fergusons in the hope of finding a clue as to her identity. If it's not even her real name, what I'm doing makes no sense, but I feel the need to keep myself busy and rooting through social media makes me feel a little less helpless. Distraction has kept me going since I woke up this morning, feeling like a ghost in my own body, and the only thing keeping me from drowning in my endless tears, is the hope that maybe in three months, I'll see her again.

"Jeff... Miss me already?" My voice is flat, and I force myself then to make more of an effort. Jeff is my only confidant since our talk in my hotel room and I appreciate him more than he knows.

"Always." He clears his throat. "Did you see the news?"

"Yes." I say, pouring myself another glass of wine. It's the first time I've drunk wine in my own bed and I'm almost ashamed to admit I still feel a little naughty about it. It's about time that I did, because being naked and tipsy under the covers is the only way to numb the emptiness I feel without her. "I watched it this morning."

"Then switch it back on. The bank we got stuck in front of yesterday..." Jeff pauses for effect. "It was robbed. Just like we thought. And guess what? I'm watching it right now, and we're on the footage. You're leaning out of the taxi window and Randy is looking furious in the front. It's hilarious!"

"Really?" I sit up and switch on the news channel, only to see the very last of it before they move onto a breaking story about a terrorist attack. I've been keeping an eye on the news online, curious about the bank incident. "I just missed it. Was anyone hurt?"

"Hurt?" Jeff laughs. "No, the bank was closed when it happened. Why do you sound so worried?"

"No reason." I try to put on a more casual tone as I continue. "So, what's the story?"

"Details are still a bit muddled," Jeff answers. "Apparently, whoever they were, they managed to disabled the alarm, then somehow managed to switch off all the security cameras. No money was stolen, but according to leaked information, a famous piece of jewelry had been taken from one of the safes. The Garamond necklace. It's made out of pink diamonds and apparently it's worth somewhere in the region of twelve million."

"Hmm... never heard of it."

"Me either, I saw it on Twitter. The owner of the necklace, a multi-media heiress, Tweeted about it. She said she was heartbroken about losing the precious piece of jewelry as it had once belonged to her mother." Jeff snorts. "She's worth over three-hundred million so I'm sure she'll get over it eventually."

"Yeah. I'm sure she will," I say absently. "And no one's been arrested yet?"

"According to the news, no. But you know, investigations tend to be kept quiet for the first few days, so it's possible." He falls silent for a moment. "How are you? Bit better than yesterday?"

"Not really," I say. "But I'll live. Just not used to feeling so miserable, that's all."

"Sorry to hear that. What are you doing?"

"Drinking wine in bed." I chuckle. "Googling her."

Jeff laughs off my self-pity. "I thought you didn't know her name."

"I don't."

"You shouldn't be drinking alone. Come out with me. It's only seven, we could get some dinner too. I'll pick you up in a taxi in an hour, how does that sound?"

I take some time to think about that. Jeff is right. It's only seven pm and I could do with the distraction because the day seems endless and I know I won't be able to sleep.

"Sure." Giving in is probably for the best. "I'll be ready."

After I hang up, I take another twenty minutes to continue with my pointless May Ferguson search. I must have gone through over seventy women with the same name when I see someone familiar looking and I hold my breath as I inch closer toward my screen. I click onto her Facebook profile. May Ferguson from Templeville, Maryland, seems like a chirpy lady. Her profile is public, allowing me to see all of it, children and friends included. It's not the woman who stole my heart; I doubt she'd post pictures of her pet gerbil named Pete, and her collection of fridge magnets, but she looks close enough to pass for her. I narrow my eyes as I pull up another picture. It's May Ferguson's official picture for her driver's license, which she apparently obtained late in life at the age of fifty. She's asking her family and friends what they think of it and there's a trail of comments underneath. I shake my head and make a mental note to check if my own profiles are set to private. Poor May Ferguson has been hacked, her identity has been stolen and she probably doesn't even know it. I have to admit, she's a smart choice. Not only does she look just like Blake but she doesn't seem to travel much, and certainly not internationally. It's unlikely someone would get caught using her identity, if they're careful.

Still not really any wiser, but feeling smug with my findings, I get out of bed and jump under the shower. As the water trickles down my back, my mind goes back to Blake, slippery and soapy against me. I think of the sounds she made when I made her come while she pulled my mouth tight against her and I take in a quick breath while my hand slides between my legs. Nothing can relieve me from the deep, sexual ache I feel as I recall the memories of those steamy nights and even my own attempts to release myself from my constant craving don't help much. As I take the showerhead out of its holder and turn up the pressure before aiming the jet between my legs, I know that these are going to be the longest three months of my life.

21

"**N**o flowers yet?" Jeff asks as he sees me lingering in the reception area. I've been down here for over three months, every day around eleven am, waiting for my daily delivery.

"No, nothing yet," I say, hopeful that the flower delivery man may have just had a flat tire, because the alternative— that something has happened to her—is unthinkable. The first bouquet of fifty perfect red roses arrived at the office the day I got back from New York and has been coming every day since. It was so big that I had to borrow a bucket from the janitors to put it in, and keep them on the floor, next to my desk. Co-workers enquired about it, but I told them I had no idea who they were from. There was no sender on the card that simply said: '*To Emily Evans*'. I knew she wanted me to know she hadn't forgotten about me, and most importantly, she wanted to let me know she was still okay. It gave me hope and got me through the awfully long days without her.

Every day before eleven I worry, and every day after the roses arrive, I feel like I can breathe again. I never thought of her as a hopeless romantic, but I love it. I bring them home with me at night, and now my small apartment is full of them, taking up the table, the kitchen counter, my night-stands, the sideboard in the hallway and even the bathroom. I bathe in them, and sometimes, when I miss her so much that I want to scream, I even sleep with them – the soft sweet petals reminding me of her skin. Instead of continuing to work at night under the bright desk light in my office like I used to, I burn candles and drink a glass of red wine on my balcony with her roses next to me while I indulge in steamy memories. I fantasize about her all the time, about what will happen if we see each other again. What she will do to me. What I will do to her. Her kiss, her touch is on my mind at all times and I often moan softly to myself, even at work. My sex drive is through the roof and I've even started dressing differently; sensual, seductive.

People around me have noticed. Anyone I work with can guess it has something to do with the roses, but they've stopped enquiring about it as they get nothing from me. I get envious looks from female colleagues and the men are simply intrigued. Although Jeff knows no more than that the flowers are sent by the woman I met in New York, it's nice to have someone who empathizes with me, and I smile as he pats my shoulder.

"Hey, don't worry about it. She probably just forgot." Rolling his eyes, he continues: "You should count yourself lucky that someone goes through the trouble of sending you flowers every day. I mean, who does that? It's been what... thirteen weeks now? Must be costing her a fortune."

"Yeah, thirteen weeks and two days." I look up when a van arrives at the gates, hopeful, but my shoulders slump when I see it's only the postman.

"Come on, Emily. This woman, whoever she is, clearly

adores you," Jeff says, lowering his voice as he pulls me into a quiet corner. "So you're still not going to tell me about her? Why the mystery? I told you all about *my* latest conquests, didn't I? Doesn't seem fair."

I chuckle and shake my head. "No, I'm still not going to tell you anything. I'm sorry, I can't."

"I can't, I can't," he repeats after me in a mocking tone. "It's all I've been getting from you lately."

I simply sigh, because there's nothing more I can say. Jeff and I have grown very close over the past months. Now that I know about his secret, I've been visiting a gay bar with him on Friday nights, acting as his wingman. We always have fun, and Jeff is considerately more outgoing in an environment where he feels safe. It's good to see him come out of his shell more and meeting men. I've now learned that Jeff grew up in a cult that claims homosexuals should be put to death and that National Geographic is a porn magazine, which explains his reluctance to come out. I've also learned he's had a rough early childhood and was placed into a good foster family at the age of twelve. I know he's tried to date women many times, but it never worked out and now that he's finally accepting himself for who he is, I think Jeff might be pretty close to happy.

Deciding I'm not going to give up, I make myself a coffee and sit down in the waiting area, suspecting I might still be there when the security guard locks the doors tonight. If Randy wants to fire me, he's welcome to do so, but I'm not going to move until I know she's okay. A feeling of unease spreads through me and I fiddle with the hem of my new pencil skirt while I try to relax into the ridiculously uncomfortable designer couch.

After only ten minutes I see someone rushing across the road with a bouquet of flowers in hand and immediately I feel better when my suspicion about the flat tire is confirmed. Getting up, I ignore my colleagues who have noticed me sitting here. Some of the envious few are perhaps hoping the whole flower spectacle will finally be over, and others like Jeff may be rooting for me. As the figure nears and I see that's it not the same delivery man but in fact, a woman, my heart starts pounding so hard I'm afraid it will fly out of my chest. There's no doubt in my mind as to who is about to walk through the rotating doors. I hold my breath as adrenaline, butterflies and intense sexual arousal, mixed with an excitement I can barely contain, all course through me at the same time. I'm breathless as my gaze follows her, and I get more and more excited when her handsome face comes sharper into focus. I want to run to her, but the shock of seeing her again is too great, too much to react to in any way other than lose myself in her blue eyes as she steps inside and spots me.

"Emily." Her voice is soothing, low, sexy, and she seems a little nervous despite her long strides and straight posture. Out of breath, she dumps her duffel bag in the middle of the reception area and smiles at me. It's not a confident smile, rather hopeful instead.

I'm frozen and can't speak.

"Sorry I'm late. I didn't want you to worry."

Jeff, the receptionist and a dozen other people follow her with their eyes as she walks up to me with the roses and hands them to me. It doesn't take much for everyone to know who sent them to me now. She's wearing jeans and a blue floral shirt and is tanned, looking like she's spent the past three months somewhere tropical, which wouldn't surprise me. Then, she gives me the same charismatic look that blew me away the first time I saw her.

I stand up on shaking legs and want to take the flowers, but more than anything, I want to kiss her. As if she's thinking the same, she tosses the flowers on the couch, closes the distance between us and throws her arms around me. She pulls me in so tight that I don't even get the chance to look at her up close before her mouth is on mine. It feels perfect and finally real as opposed to my many fantasies. I love her impatience; her lips are determined and hungry, parting my mouth and as her tongue finds mine, I wrap my arms around her too, sinking into the kiss that sets us both on fire. Drowning in a blissful haze, I forget about everything and everyone around me. I move my hands down her back and slip them underneath her shirt, then run them up her spine. After all this time of longing for her, the softness of her skin and her body pressing tight against mine are making me so aroused that I have to pace myself. I want her like I've never wanted anything. A moan escapes her, and I can sense from her tightening muscles that she feels the same. It's awfully quiet around us and I chuckle as I pull out of the kiss, conscious that everyone is staring at us. Emily Evans kissing a woman is the last thing they expected to see, but I don't care. All I care about is her being back in my life.

"You found me." My words are barely a whisper and I gather all my willpower not to kiss her again as she smiles and stares down at my mouth before meeting my eyes, breathing fast.

"Of course I found you." She brushes a lock of hair away from my face in a gesture so tender that I cover her hand with my own, pressing it against my cheek as I let out a deep sigh. "I would have found you anywhere."

"I know. Let's go somewhere else," I say. "I want to be alone with you."

She takes my hand and it feels perfect in mine. Before we leave, I grab the roses. They're the last ones after all, and I want to make good memories with them.

"Emily, what is this nonsense and where do you think you're going?" I turn to find Randy standing beside me with a coffee cup in one hand and a notepad in the other. "Our twelve o'clock is here, waiting in the meeting room."

I almost laugh when I notice everyone is holding their breath as the great Randy tries to publicly humiliate me. "I'm leaving," I say as I tighten my grip on Blake's hand. "I've had enough of this place."

Randy's face turns a dark shade of crimson when some of my co-workers quietly chuckle. "You can't do that. It's..." His voice trails off when Blake gives him a stare that would even scare me if I didn't know better. She doesn't need words to communicate, her body language says it all and I can tell Randy feels intimidated by her.

I turn my back on him and give Jeff a long hug, because I know I might not see him in a while and I'm going to miss him. "Take care, I'll call you," I whisper, ignoring everyone else. Then I reach for Blake's hand again and when we walk out the door together, I know I've never been more ready for my new life to start.

22

"Let's go to my place," I say as I drive toward town. My hand is still clenching hers in the car, resting on my thigh as if I'm afraid she'll disappear again if I don't hold onto it. I can barely concentrate on the road. Twice, I drive through a red light and only just dodge a cyclist as I turn into the drive of my apartment building, desperate to be alone with her. My mind is consumed with fantasies, my body restless and filled with anticipation.

Walking from the car to my front door, she puts an arm around me, and it puts me at ease because I know then that she's here to stay. That she's been waiting and wanting this too, missing me just as much as I've missed her.

"I see you like my roses," she says as she walks in and looks around.

"I do. I love them." I've been adding rose food and so they easily last for up to ten days. The five-hundred stems spread throughout the rooms are an impressive, impactful sight and I can tell by the look on her face she didn't expect to see this. She traces a finger along the row of vases in the hallway and follows me into the open kitchen and living room, where more roses are on display. I've used an old aquarium, big jars, a watering jug and even my grandmother's old teapot to keep them in after running out of vases. On the blackboard above the kitchen table, the cards that came with the flowers are secured with magnets in neat rows. They're all the same; white with gold text printed on them. I like how the light reflects on the gold foil at night, lighting up my name almost a hundred times. The roses and the cards make me feel special, and it makes my apartment look pretty too; like an old Parisian studio, rather than a soulless new build in the suburbs of Phoenix.

Opening the fridge, I scan the side rack for beverages. There's an unopened bottle of Chablis and half a bottle of gin. Now that she's here, I'm jittery and in need of something to do.

"Drink?" I ask, feeling silly because I know a drink is the last thing on our minds right now.

"No, I don't want a drink," she says matter-of-factly, then tilts her head and studies me as I close the fridge and turn around to face her. I can tell she likes what I'm wearing. Black pencil skirts, high heels and white satin blouses have been my uniform at work lately. It's decent enough for a meeting but I also know it looks very sexy on me, with the long split over my right leg and my thigh-high stockings underneath. They're only slightly visible when I sit down and cross my legs, but I made sure she saw I was wearing them in the car.

"Good," I agree. "Because I don't want a drink either. I want you."

She comes closer and I step back until my backside meets the kitchen counter. A grin spreads across her face as she leans in and runs her thumb over my lips. I part them, take her hand and suck it into my mouth, drawing a quick breath from her. The pull between us is insanely powerful and magnetic, and the heat of our chemistry sets us both on fire when her hands slide over my hips and cups my ass in a possessive hold. I moan and she responds by taking the hem of my skirt, pulling it up a little until the edge of my thigh-high stocking becomes visible. I'm so wet and the constant pulse between my legs has only grown during the drive here. I know that if she as much as touches me there, I will come. Her gaze is oozing desire, as she yanks my skirt further up to my waist and presses me against the counter with her thigh between my legs. The long kiss that follows makes me groan and buck my hips against her. I reach out to unbutton her shirt because I want to feel her skin against mine, but she takes my wrists and with one hand, holds them on the counter behind me.

"Later," she whispers in a low voice, her lips barely brushing mine as she speaks. I gasp at the overwhelming craving for her mouth and lean in to kiss her. She pulls back and lets her eyes roam over me as she trails a hand down to the edge of my stockings, then continues up my inner thigh.

It's hard to keep my balance in the black stiletto heels, the way my legs are trembling, but she holds me up with her body that she presses against me. She spreads my legs with her thigh, and the pressure of her hip against my pussy almost makes me come.

"Oh God, I love it when you do that" I mutter as my breath quickens. My words encourage her to rip open my blouse, too impatient to bother with the buttons. I cry out when she pulls down my red, lace bra to envelop my nipple with her warm mouth. I've missed the delightful shooting pains that bring me to the edge of ecstasy when she bites me, and by now, my matching red panties are coated with my juices. Moving her mouth to my neck, she sucks at my skin until a thrilling sting makes me gasp. I'm desperate to run my hands over her body in return, but she continues to hold me in her grip. Even now, after longing for each other for months, she still can't resist teasing me and I wonder where she gets the willpower from because right now, I don't want to take it slow.

"I need you to make me come," I say, breathing fast. Her pupils are dilated and the desire in her eyes is making me twitch. My brain is overloaded by pleasure, almost too much to handle. Deciding I've been teased long enough, she slides her hand down my body and slips it into the front of my panties, groaning when she feels how wet I am for her.

"God, Emily. I love how much you want me." Bringing her lips to my ear, she continues: "I've been dreaming about fucking you for ninety-five days, dying to be inside you, to taste you. Do you have any idea what that does to a person?"

"I know exactly how it feels," I whisper, my words catching as she brushes her thumb across my clit. Unable to hold back any longer, and clearly in need of release herself, she starts riding my thigh while she enters me deeply and we moan against each other's lips. Her two fingers filling me up causes my body to convulse and when she adds a third, we're both completely delirious and it doesn't take much for her to start shaking against me. The sudden shift in energy causes her to let go of my hands and I immediately reach for her face and pull her tighter against my mouth as she fucks me hard and fast, lacing the fingers of her free hand through my hair.

"Come with me, Emily," she says, before we shatter into a million pieces together. As she cries out, I hear myself screaming her name for the first time.

23

The sun has set, and the candles burning on my nightstands cast a cozy glow over my warm red bedroom walls. Although it's a strange color for a bedroom, it works, and it gives the space a sexy and intimate feel. Last week I felt a sudden urge to redecorate, in need of more red in my life. I guess the roses inspired me to do that.

We're in bed, under the covers, making out in each other's arms like we're teenagers. I don't know how long we've been here, but I can't seem to get enough of it, and neither can Blake. Her lips feel perfect against mine, her tongue incredible, and now that we know we have more time, we cherish the closeness after an afternoon of hot, steamy sex.

Take-out boxes are on the floor next to the bed, along with an empty bottle of white wine. I know there is no way we will be leaving the bed in the next couple of days, even though we haven't discussed what we're going to do yet. I can feel in her kiss that she's not going to leave me again and that's enough to put me at ease. We both know we need to talk, but the serious stuff can wait, this feels too good not to do right now. Our limbs are entangled, our bodies pressed together as she lies half on top of me. I feel complete, happy and spent, yet arousal still tugs at me each time she shifts to roam her hands over my body, and each time I touch her in return. Blake is incredible in every way and I want her in my arms forever. Her full breasts, her broad shoulders, her muscular thighs, her incredible smile... And then there's her laugh. It's warm, infectious, boisterous, and it triggers an emotion in me so raw, that my skin tightens, and I feel light-headed with happiness. I could spend all day just listening to her laugh.

I trail my hand down along her waist and hips, then along the inside of her thigh. Her breath catches when I move further up and feel how wet she still is. Knowing she wants me turns up the heat in me each time I feel it.

"Wait," she says, taking my wrist, stopping me from going any further. Then she leans over, zips open her duffel bag on the floor and takes out her strap-on. I suck in a quick breath as I watch her put it on, my pulse suddenly jittering somewhere in the 160 range. She has that look in her eyes again. It's a look of promise, need, anticipation, and very, very sexy thoughts. Sitting on the edge of the bed, she leans back on her hands and waits.

"What do you want?" I ask her, already knowing the answer.

"Straddle me," she says, then bites her lip, looking me up and down.

I crawl over and swing one leg over her, then wrap my arms around her neck as I raise myself onto my knees. My breasts are aligned with her face and I shiver when her breath washes over them. Her lips brush them softly before her tongue takes over, circling my rock-hard nipples and I buck my hips against her stomach. I want her inside me so badly, I can hardly wait. Her hands close around my hips, guiding me to where she wants me. The tip of the shaft pushes against me and I tremble in delight as I lower myself and feel it filling me, little by little. I close my eyes and wait for a moment as it feels so tight that it almost hurts, then continue when my pussy is aching for more.

"Good girl." Blake knows exactly how to push my buttons, and I see a glimmer in her eyes at my reaction to her words.

"God, you feel amazing," I whisper when I lower myself completely onto her lap. It's tight, crazy good and I can already feel a tingle spreading out from my core as I weave my hands through her silky hair that's now a shade lighter from the sunshine she's been exposed to.

"Fuck," she curses, lifting her hips. She is so deep, and I can see she's wild with desire as I start rocking back and forth on her lap, slowly at first. I know the friction feels good to her, so I thrust forward harder and faster. I can make her come whenever I please now and that arouses me even more.

Overcome by a sudden surge of power, I push her back into the mattress and smile at the surprised expression on her face. I can see she didn't expect me to take over, but she's too turned on to protest. I lean forward and take her wrists, then place them above her head, holding onto them as I ride her faster and harder. My climax builds like a raging storm inside me and from the look on her face, I know she's on the edge too. Her teeth are clenched and the sexy frown between her brows grows deeper as a deep growl escapes her.

"I want you to come," I say, and she loses it, lifting her hips up against me, over and over until I fall on top of her and let go while I cry out. Her arms are around me now, pulling me closer as she thrust into me, sending a wave of aftershocks through my core. I shiver each time one hits me, and when my muscles finally start to relax we both let out a deep, satisfied sigh

"What was that?" Blake asks, arching a brow for comical effect. Her hair is messy and it looks cute, the way it sticks out on all sides.

"I don't know," I say honestly, and laugh. "You make me crazy. Good crazy, though."

A smile paints her face, and millions of butterflies start flapping around in my stomach, making me weak in every single limb. The effect she has on me is beyond my comprehension, but I have stopped analyzing my physical reactions to her and just enjoy the ride now, because there is more than enough time for that later.

"I can't deny it was good, Miss Evans, but I might have to punish you for taking advantage of me in a vulnerable moment. Remember, you're not the one in charge here, I am." She grins, then turns us over so she's on top. She's still inside me and I moan when she spreads my legs with her own and pushes into me while she grabs my wrists in the same manner. I love it when she does that, and I want nothing more than for her to take me again.

"This isn't exactly punishment," I reply through quick breaths, wrapping my legs around her hips.

"Maybe not right now." She kisses my neck up to my ear and rests her mouth there before she continues while pulling out of me. "But believe me, I'm going to make you beg."

24

"Are you tired? When I open my eyes, Blake stands over me with a rose in her hand and trails it along my breasts. My nipples harden at the touch and I shiver as she continues down and rests it between my legs. "I've filled the tub. Want to come in with me?"

"Of course, I say." I was asleep but the thought of taking a hot, relaxing bath with her sounds like a dream, and I sit up, rolling my shoulders and rubbing my tired eyes. Blake wasn't joking when she said she would make me beg. She teased me for hours, keeping me on the edge of an orgasm until I couldn't take it anymore. The result was rewarding, and I can barely breathe as I think back to the moment that she finally let me go, taking me from behind while my wrists were tied together behind my back. I've never felt anything like it, and still, when the vision flashes across my mind's eye, my pussy twitches like it hasn't been touched in months.

When I step into the bathroom, there are candles and roses scattered around the edge of the tub, on the shelves, on the windowsill, and on the laundry basket. She's switched the lights off, and the faint flickering of the candles is reflected in the big mirror above the basin. Steam is misting over the tub and on top fragrant rose petals are floating, covering the surface of the water. I've never been a sucker for romance, but since meeting Blake, I want it all. I step into the tub and wait for her to get in between my legs. When she sits down, I pull her closer and let out a deep breath when she places her head against my shoulder. Her body against mine feels right, perfect, just the way it should be. My arm wraps around her as I run my other hand through her hair, and she closes her eyes with a contented sigh. I love to stroke her hair, and I have a feeling I'm about to find many more little things I love to do to her. Still puzzled as to how it happened, I know she not only owns me sexually, but she has my mind and my heart too. All of me.

"So what do we do now?" I ask. The day and the evening have been more perfect than I could ever have imagined but now seems like a good time to discuss things while we are simply relaxing together.

"What do you want to do?" She asks in return.

"You don't have any plans?" I smile because I like where this is heading. "Will you take me with you this time?"

"Of course." She turns her head and kisses my neck. "I need to pick up my passport in New Mexico first, but after that we can go anywhere you want."

"Your passport? What name will be on there?"

"Blake Howard." Her hands stroke my thighs and rest on my knees. "I'm going to be myself again. It's a fresh start, yet familiar in so many ways."

"Blake Howard," I repeat. "I like it. Did you grow up in New Mexico?"

"Yeah. In a town called Red River. It's pretty, I think

you'll like it. I still have a house there. It might be falling apart by now, but I'm sure the safe is still in my office because I've been pretty thorough with the security."

"So you'll take me there first?" My heart sings at the thought of visiting her hometown together. Knowing more about her makes me feel closer to her, and I need that more than anything.

"Yeah, I'd like you to come with me." Her voice is sweet, not a trace of her usual dominance in it. "And after that, it's up to you."

"Hmmm... anywhere, huh?" I say with a dreamy look in my eyes. "How about Hawaii?"

"If you want."

"Or the Seychelles?"

"We could go there."

"Where do you want to live?" I ask. "I can't imagine you've had any place you've called home over the past few years. Is there a place you've always wanted to live?"

She thinks about that for a moment and sighs. "Well... there was this place in Key West where I did a job, years ago. I rented a house close by. I really liked it there, so much so that I almost forgot I was there to work. The beach is beautiful, and it was the only place I ever regretted leaving.

"Sounds nice." I hesitate, then decide to ask the question that's been bugging me straight-out. "So you robbed a bank in Key West?"

"How do you know about the banks?" Blake looks up with a puzzled and somewhat worried look.

"I put two and two together, in New York. That was a bank, wasn't it? In Midtown East? I just couldn't figure out why you risked coming back to my room." I cast my gaze over the roses. "But I think I get it now." When my hand skims her cheek, I feel a tear. "You really care about me."

She nods, then turns further to look into my eyes. For a moment, I see hesitation, but the words that come out are nothing but sincere. "I love you, Emily."

I melt at her words and a lump settles in my throat. Never had I expected them to come from her, but something has broken her hard exterior and I can finally see through the armor. The earnest expression in her eyes brings tears to my own and I have to swallow hard before I can answer her. "I love you too, Blake," I whisper, and kiss her softly. A warm glow spreads through me at the light touch of her lips and I know I need her in my life forever. This is not a fleeting thing, a moment of passion. It's not about sex or exploring my fantasies and it's not about escaping boredom or the need to break free from my mundane life. It's about Blake, about us. I'm terrified and hopeful at the same time, because I know that as long as I'm with her, everything will be fine. Overwhelmed by feelings so intense that I couldn't name them if I tried, I'm ready for whatever she has to offer. Pulling her closer, I whisper: "Let's go to Key West."

25

"You know you won't need much more than a bikini, right?" Blake laughs at the four large suitcases I've packed. "Or you could just walk around naked, I'm fine with that too."

"I know you are. But I need some clothes to wear at some point." I roll my eyes and chuckle as we start loading my stuff into the trunk of my car. After three days in bed, it's time to leave and I'm buzzing with excitement. Besides being all over each other, we've talked a lot and by now, I know more about her than I know about my friends or family. Her favorite music, food, places, her fears hopes and dreams, her childhood, her interests and she's even told me a few things about her 'side job' as she calls it, and the six million dollars scattered over several of her bank accounts across the world. She also told me about her three months spent holed up in Salvador, Brazil. Apparently, it's a great city to disappear in, with almost two million inhabitants. In return, I've answered all Blake's questions and, although she doesn't seem to agree, I've come to the conclusion that I'm terribly dull and need to do something about that. It's time to live.

"Yes, you're right. You probably do need some clothes for when I take you to dinner or out in our new boat." She smiles as she pushes the last case on top of the others. "You told me you like boats, so we'll get one. I think Emily is an excellent name for a boat, don't you?"

"Really?" I grin as I wrap my arms around her, and she laughs as she pushes me against the car and leans into me. What starts out as an innocent kiss soon turns heated, and we pull apart breathless when one of my neighbors walks by. "I'd love that," I whisper, and remove the red lipstick traces from her mouth.

I've been packing all day and the sun is low now. Fall has started but it's still warm, and I wipe the sweat off my brow as I turn to look up at my apartment one last time. I won't miss it; I won't miss anything. Renting it out can be dealt with later, but right now, I just want to leave with her.

"Are you ready?" she asks. "Because I want to show you something before the sun goes down. I figured you might want to say goodbye to your city."

"I'm intrigued. What is it?"

"You'll have to wait and see so let me drive, I'll take you there," she says, playfully snatching the car keys from my hand.

After parking the car in downtown Phoenix, I'm surprised to find her leading me to the Chase Tower, the tallest skyscraper in Arizona. It's the city's pride and joy, but as it houses offices, I've never been up there.

"Come on, we have to hurry." She takes my hand and we

head for the North entrance, where I wait in the reception area as she talks to the security guard by the door. They seem to exchange jokes because I hear them laugh, and I wonder why she's taking her time talking with him while she told me to rush. A little later, she's back and nods toward the elevators.

"We can't just go up there," I whisper.

"You're right, we're not supposed to but we're going up anyway." She winks as she holds up a key card that she uses to call the elevator.

"Did you just steal that from him?" I ask, keeping my voice down.

"This is where magic comes in handy."

"Magic? Pickpocketing you mean?"

"It's all the same." She shrugs as if what we're doing is nothing. I suppose compared to robbing a bank it's not a big deal, but I still feel uneasy as we get in and she presses the button for the thirty-eighth floor. "Don't worry, we're safe. I gave him the name of some mid-level manager who looks vaguely like me and said I forgot something upstairs. I noticed he was sports betting on his phone, so we talked about baseball while I removed the key card from his lanyard. He won't be missing it for a while, he told me he'd just ordered a pizza."

Despite my nerves, I laugh. "I'm impressed, seeing you in action first-hand. You're good, it's very sexy."

"Oh yeah?" She inches closer and walks me back until I'm cornered, then presses her lips to mine. Her breath, her warmth, her body, her want that draws me in and the sexual energy that radiates between us; I'm aware of everything. I'm also aware of the security camera, but her mouth is impossible to resist, and I give in to her by parting my lips, inviting her in. Before I know it, my fingers are running through her hair and her hands are on my behind, pulling me against her hips with an urgent need. As always, the kiss turns heated and steals my breath and it is nearly impossible to stop I'm so crazy for her. The caress of her lips and her tongue makes me quiver and I let out a muttered curse of disappointment when the lift doors open.

"Fuck." I shake my head and smile because I can see she doesn't want to stop either. Pressing the emergency button will most likely get us arrested though, so we break apart and reluctantly get out.

There are two more floors to walk via the concrete staircase next to the elevator and I know her eyes are on my behind as I climb ahead of her, my short, teal dress giving her a perfect view of my panties. I like it when Blake watches me. It turns me on and if we weren't chasing a sunset right now, I'd stop, rid myself of my dress and let her have her way with me right here on the staircase.

'Later', I tell myself, because I know we will have all the time in the world. We're not even sure where we're going to end up yet, after we've visited New Mexico. Key West is part of the plan, but who knows what we'll find on our way there? Right now, the world is our oyster and I want to make love to her in each town we pass, no matter how small. I love her so wholly, so passionately that I wonder if there are other people in this world who have felt the same. Perhaps this feeling of all-encompassing obsessive desire and love is what has shaped the greatest art. If I had any talent on that front, I'd paint her a picture or write her a song but even then, it would never come close to expressing how I feel because she's everything to me.

. . .

U p on the fortieth floor, which is a dark and noisy mechanical level, she uses my hairpin to unlock the heavy door leading to the roof. When we step out, I have to blink a couple of times, almost blinded by the most magnificent sunset that welcomes us. It's a little scary as there's no railing but we sit down a couple of feet from the edge and look out over the city that is glowing in orange light. It's so pretty and for the first time, I truly appreciate the urban landscape and the majesty of the sun like never before. The buildings are illuminated by the sun sinking behind them and slithers of pink dance over the sky as they fade into the night.

"This is incredible," I whisper, leaning into her as she puts an arm around me. I've forgotten all about our illegal break-in, and enjoying the view and her closeness is all I want to do in this moment. The setting is so romantic, so perfect, that I feel like my heart will burst.

"It is." Blake places a kiss on my temple, and a shiver runs through me. I feel so much, it's insane. "You know we can come back whenever you want, right?" she continues. "I don't want you to feel like your life has been ripped away from you, and besides, your parents will miss you."

"I know. I'll call them and let them know I'm fine." I want to tell her that she is my life, that I don't need anything apart from her, but I think she already knows that her soul is now inextricably intertwined with mine. Blake has woken me up and this is not a dream anymore. "Thank you for bringing me here. It's the perfect goodbye," I say instead as I turn to look at her. The last light of the day casts a dim glow over her features and instead of looking at the beautiful sunset taking place before me, my eyes are unable to leave her because she's so attractive, it's addictive. In that moment, I decide I have to have her, no matter what. Her body is like a magnet, luring me in with an almost crackling static.

"How long do we have?" I ask, pushing her down gently against the concrete base before lifting my skirt and crawling on top of her.

"Twenty minutes, max." She doesn't fight it, just looks up at me with eagerness in her gaze.

"Let me," I say. "I want to make you feel good. She complies when I unbuckle her belt and open the button and the zipper of her jeans, before laying down on top of her. "I want you." Her hands reach for me, but I take them and place them next to her head. "Just let me." My voice is soft and again, she complies, as if she's decided we've played enough games, or perhaps she sees no reason to object because she wants me as much as I want her. When I reach down into her jeans and feel how much she craves me, a moan slips from both our lips. In an instant, her hips jerk up, needing my touch, and I know that this is no time to tease her. My fingers skim her hard, throbbing clit, making her groan and I kiss her so fiercely I'm afraid I'll suffocate us both. As darkness falls and the colors of the pink-tinged twilight on the horizon slowly dissipate, her moans grow louder. I regret the night now, not being able to see her face in sharp focus because I know it's painted with need. My fingers are on her, slipping through her wet folds and circling her clit until she bucks her hips and cries my name in a crazy frenzy that echoes across the roof. It's exhilarating, the way she gives in to me, so wholly, so completely.

"Emily," she says again, this time in a whimper as she wraps her arms around me. "Fuck..." Aftershocks make her tremble and I watch her eyelids flutter, opening and closing in time to the rhythm of my heartbeat. When she exhales deeply, a content softness spreads across her face, and I cannot resist kissing her. The day has ended, and our new life is about to begin.

AFTERWORD

I hope you've loved reading *The Good Girl* as much as I've loved writing it. If you've enjoyed this book, would you consider rating it and reviewing it on www.amazon.com? Reviews are very important to authors and I'd be really grateful, especially as this is my first novella :)